Timothy Harada is a Native American/Buddhist, singer/songwriter and activist. He is an honors graduate from the first graduating class of the new Soka University of America, in Orange County, California. Along with writing music, poetry and books, Timothy records music, and he plays saxophone, guitar and piano. Many of the songs from Timothy's CDs have been played on radio stations in Japan and the US. Though Timothy was raised in Orange County, California, he is now performing in Sendai, Japan, where he lives with his Japanese wife. Timothy has now also released the first 3 volumes of his *Collected Writings From Soka University of America*, which are out on paperback. Many of Timothy's original works can be seen or heard on his website:

www.timharada.com

Myth Shattering

Myth Shattering

A Novel

Timothy Harada

Second American Renaissance Press

Second American Renaissance Press
471 Adams Ave.
Escondido CA 92026

978-0-6151-8685-6
3rd Edition

Second American Renaissance Press
1st International paperback printing: March 2007.
Printed in the United States of America.

Cover painting: The unfinished work of Michael Godard.

For more works by this author see www.timharada.com

Other works by Timothy Harada Include:

Love: The Only Proven Way to Fight Terrorism (CD)
Acts of Sedition: Classified CIA Files (CD)
The Collected Writings From Soka University of America, Volume 1-3 (Books)

I dedicate this book to my mentor in life, Daisaku Ikeda (the greatest writer I've ever known), and to the hundreds of thousands of people around the world, who in 2002 and 2003 didn't buy the lies of the unelected man from Texas-those who came out in unprecedented numbers to march in the streets around the world, to say no to his planned illegal, illegitimate, and immoral war on the people of Iraq. We didn't believe his lies then, and we still don't believe his lies now.

Although we didn't stop him from carrying out his devilish plans, we stripped him of any legitimacy to wage a barbaric war on an already destroyed (thanks to the first gulf war and 10 plus years of US sanctions) and defenseless nation that, as we were screaming in the streets at the time, "had nothing to do with September 11th." We were right then, and now the whole world knows it.

There is a great divide in the world today, which is all too evident in the US. It is not a divide between ideologies or between religious differences-it is, as Howard Zinn points out, a divide between public opinion and government policy. The rulers of the world in most countries do not even slightly represent the will of their people, and in the US, they are so far removed from representing the people's will. The leaders of the US, the UK, Japan, Italy, and a few others nations defied the will of their people and the will of people around the world, in supporting Bush's illegal war against UN resolutions. Now, some of those governments, even after all of Bush lies have been exposed, still go against the will of their people by continuing to support a war that never should have happened, and needs to end now.

When will our leaders learn as Sting sings in his famous song, Russians, *"There's no such thing as a winnable war; it a lie we don't believe any more."*

Thank you for picking up this book, Timothy Harada

This novel is based on true stories.
Most of the names have been changed to protect the innocent and the guilty alike.

Prelude

The field was empty. The only animate life, which stirred, was a joyful grasshopper dancing on a newly sheered lawn. She danced, oblivious to her onlooker-the shrewd officer Sajack, who sat guard in his revving patrol/golf cart as it belched noxious exhaust fumes into the sweet smelling September ocean breeze.

Sajack was stationed at the western most corner of the school's athletic field. He vigilantly displayed his honorary rent-a-cop talents, lest any devious skater should violate the city's newest in a million worthless ordinances, banning the use of skate boards in public-or was it just on the sidewalks and city streets? But then where else would they skate? Or should he be so lucky to, on this the first day of school, catch a vile escapee who tempts to leave the compound before the last class is dismissed.

It seemed the laws grew stricter and stricter, month after month, year after year. As if with a mind of their own, they tried fecklessly to keep abreast with the local paper's boast of this being "the safest city in America!" I guess, it just depends on whose side you're on.

With only a few minutes left before the grand bell tower blared out "The Chimes of Westminster," signaling the student's departure, this ever-ready narcotics officer ("Nark Spoogwak," as the kids tagged him) waited in weary anticipation, afraid his day might have been better spent employing his time in the local doughnut shop. But he was determined before the day was up to catch "some little punk" lighting up a cigarette, or heaven forbid crossing the street between the two controlled intersections that hugged the campus on both north and south.

In direct response to the city government's ever-growing oppressiveness, the kids grew year by year more defiant. Like weeds that break though the city streets, they proved the forces of life only grow stronger against the countervailing forces, which attempt to suppress them.

He felt little honor keeping watch over a section of the city's greatest historical landmarks. Built in 1908, this high school with its double-decker auditorium, newly remodeled coliseum style football stadium, and once filled Olympic size pool-now drained like the city's budget, thanks to the newest addition to the police station's arsenal of "peace keeping" devices (the Bell, Notar Chopper.) This mammoth buzzard is but one of the two police helicopters, which can be heard on any street corner and into the wee hours of the night circling over head- sure to disturb anyone's peace should they try to enjoy a salubrious picnic in central park, or nap on the beach on a Saturday afternoon.

In the brief moment of silence before the bells chimed, officer Sajack had a slight instance of introspection. As the sun beat down on his black, soiled "D.A.R.E." cap, causing perspiration to trickle down his long forehead, he heard the voice of his father echoing in his memory: "What do you want to do with your Life..Life..Life...."

***

The largest profession in this city was membership to the boy's club style, omnipresent police force. Any tourist visiting downtown wouldn't have to be foolish to believe that there were at least one or two officers per capita. Anywhere anyone was willing to display openly his or her free spirit, a cop was surely there to repress it.

Sajack failed entry-level admissions testing into the ominous police academy due to his weak physical strength, which had been worsening ever since his knee injury five years prior, in his short lived junior college football career. But he wouldn't give up on his dreams of wearing a real badge and carrying a "real man's" gun. And thanks to his few years experience as a security guard at the local mall, and his high school brainwashing in Jr. ROTC, he landed this job, "babysitting snotty nose kids" as he called it. He knew he would have to pay his dues to see those dreams materialize.

***

In the height of meditation he was suddenly awoken by a heralding: "DING!!! DONG!!! DING!!! DONG!!!"

The whole town was accustomed to this hourly song, a tribute to that ragged European Empire, whose folly the city and state's elites tried desperately to emulate. The people of this city wouldn't even need a watch. After the "Chimes of Westminster," the bells would sound out the number of hours past in the day. As the number of chimes grew, so did the victims of this city's authoritarian guards.

It was with this cacophonous toll that the kids gushed from their classrooms, pouring down the stairways like an over-flowing underground eruption.

***

The student body of Wutherington Beach High, all glazed eyed, the descendants of those greedy "Manifest Destiny" touting, robber barrens, who stole this fertile land of "Alta California" some one and a half centuries ago, from Mexico and from other hapless natives.

Though this state bore little resemblance to her past history, the karmic retributions of their forefather's thievery were still being strongly felt. The two plates of land still grinding up against each other at the so-called "San Andreas Fault" shook frequently. A state of once massive wetlands, covered by thirsty land developers, caused a year-by-year increase in flooding. A corporate prison industrial complex growing like a tumor at a ferocious pace infected and devoured whole segments of the so-called "underclass" youths, whom incarcerated made easy targets for corporate America's revisited attempts at slave labor. And with a gaping hole in the ozone, and increased green house gases, the summer heat seemed to grow almost intolerable at times, and caused a change in climate at a rate unparalleled in human history.

This "dream land" was once thought by Cortez's men to be the island of "Califia." Now this land of *Atzlan* far better resembled a volcano ready to explode. From where would a solution be found to this society's many quandaries? Who would rise from this swampland of growing despair and offer the fresh fragrant wisdom so needed by the people?

The First Day

"Yo, Nate! What are you trying to beat everyone home to do your homework? You can't even fuckin' read!" Debussy called across the street to his friend Nathan, who was walking faster than usual.

"Shit, get your ugly ass over here! What, do I have to fuckin' baby-sit you again this year?" He responded jokingly. The two boys always walked home together last year, while in middle school. Nathan never expected life to be any different this year.

Debussy darted across the street, hoping Sajack wasn't in view, and with a loud hollow "thud" sound, limpyed Nathan on the back of the head. Nathan quickly responded by giving Debussy a Charley horse.

"Dude, did you see Lori Thompson in history class?" laughing off the soreness in his leg, Debussy reminisced, smiling devouringly.

"I know; shit it's a wonder what the California sun can do to a chick's tits over the summer." He answered, gesticulating with his hands in front of his chest. "Yeah, watermelons are sure in season this year!"

Giggling loudly, they kept commenting down Main Street about their first day of high school. Both boys were quite tanned, having spent most of their summer breaks at the beach, body surfing and skateboarding. They resented not being able to bring their skateboards to school this year, especially with a farther walk home than last year.

"Why isn't Chris with you?"

"We're gonna meet him at Lake Park." Answered Nathan, nonchalantly.

"Are you guys gonna smoke some bud or what?" Debussy didn't seem as interested as last year.

"What you got the Mott's?"

"Shit, you stoned or just stupid? What, the summer sun dried up your brain juice, made you forget how to walk walls?" Joked Debussy.

"No; just thought I'd save some sweat, Dweeb."

The boys never bought their herb. It was in ample supply in most backyards, and they were experts at borrowing from their neighbors. Nevertheless, Nathan Phelps was always trying to get Debussy Jensen and Christopher Andrews to do all the dirty work, while bathing in all the unwarranted reward.

Nathan was, despite his lack of intelligence, an instinctively brilliant conman, who could, with his overt ignorance, make anyone feel sorry for him, unless they helped him out. He was a fairly good-looking straight, sandy blond haired, (except when he dyed it and put it up in "liberty spikes," to shock his teachers, parents, and friends) husky built kid, who believed religiously: "Rules are made for young boys to find a way around."

A modern day Huck Finn, or Dennis the Menace, he tried in every possible way to convert other kids to the ways of his religious convictions, and tried to get them to do his bidding. In a troglodytic way, he walked with his head bent forward, slightly hunched back, with his pants sagging down, somewhat revealing the crack of his rear end.

Neither he nor any of his acolytes carried books home, and he didn't intend on doing any homework-another one of those rules he cleverly avoided. However, he somehow managed to make it all the way to high school, by either looking off a classmate's papers, or by making some weaker kid do his assignments.

Debussy had the brains in the group, though he didn't let the others know. Up until then, he was the pacifist, who just went along with Nathan's ploys, to avoid a fight. He was quite a bit thinner than Nathan, and had no inclination to push anyone around, even if he could. He had a glowing face, with hazel-brown eyes, which always showed a sign of compassion. He had wavy, blond hair. (Though on occasion, he had it Depped up in spikes, and seldom dyed it odd colors to give it a little shock value.) Both boys wore studded earrings in their left ears, and at times, long dangling ones, adorned with anarchy symbols or spiked balls-anything to get people's attention.

His friends called him "Debut"-an honorary title, attributed in part to his originality. He was a new breed of X'ers. He often signed his name "Debut X"-the last name a play-on-words, a reversal of Malcolm X's idea (where Malcolm couldn't possibly know his father's ancestral name, thanks to slavery, Debussy asserted "Having been raised by a long line of mothers, who had to give up their names to patriarchy, how could I possibly know my real name?") He boasted, if he ever got married, he would definitely take his wife's name.

Secondly, the "X" was a sign of his growing belief, that he would be the only redeeming voice of his forgotten, downsized, X'ed-out generation. He was a radically free thinker, often to an exaggerated degree. A modern day Socratic "gad fly," he loved to defy convention and question reality.

Lastly the "X" stood for his dead father's last name, Xanthankis, which he could only use in secrecy, which his mother X'ed out when Mr. Xanthankis left this world for greener pastures.

As they crossed the street to Lake Park, Nathan gave Debussy a "flat tire." Debussy tried getting Nathan back by sticking his leg out to trip him. Unfortunately, as Nathan would have done the same thing, he instinctively saw it coming.

"Yeah right! I'm not as dumb as you look. Think I'm gonna fall for that crap?" But as Nathan walked backward, laughing at Debussy, who struggled to put his shoe back on, Nathan wasn't paying attention to the curb, which he was heading straight for. Consequently, he tripped flat on his back in the damp grass of Lake Park.

Christopher, who sat waiting on a park bench, seized the opportunity, while Nathan was down, to run up and limpy him on the head. Laughing, Christopher ran off through the park, as Nathan tried to chase him.

Nathan was the slowest amongst the three. Christopher knew he couldn't possibly catch up. Despite his Asthma, Christopher ran circles around Nathan, cracking up hysterically. However, as Christopher was only paying attention to his temporary opponent (and there were never, as a rule, any set teams in horseplay), Debussy approached from behind and kicked one of Christopher's legs out behind the other. He brought Christopher down into the dampened grass, where both boys dog-piled on top. Then due to his weight, Nathan managed to get atop and started dead legging his two opponents. Finally, when Nathan felt too tired, he rolled off and said, as if nothing had happened, "OK, you wimps! Get off your ugly asses and let's get stoned!" They all got up laughing, repeating the mantra "Let's get stoned! Let's get stoned!"

Christopher did it out of a sense of coercion, Debussy out of a force of habit. Both were less enthused than Nathan, who would smoke pot 24 hours a day, if only he had the resources. Though due to his lazy nature, he never would.

Although Christopher and Debussy were hurting a little from being under Nathan's weight, it wasn't considered "cool" to show any pain or hold any grudges. Christopher also had to hide the fact that he was sort of pissed his new pants had gotten soiled. He knew Nathan would only make fun of him. He was the only one whose family could afford such nice clothes.

Nathan called Christopher "preppy boy," because the latter's pants were never frayed at the bottom, like the formers. Both Nathan and Debussy would simply put together flannels and jeans from different thrift and second hand stores to have clothes to wear for school.

Walking Walls

As soon as they walked through the park and through some tracked houses, they climbed concrete walls that separated the yards of each house that circled the park. They were seasoned "wall walkers," who could even run the walls, if the job called for it. Both Debussy and Christopher could beat Nathan cold getting atop the wall. Though once Nathan got up, he fared pretty well staying abreast with the other two.

Debussy usually walked in the forefront, while Nathan made a great caboose. Nathan was always ready to smart off with anyone who tried to give them any trouble for trespassing. Once he told off an old man who yelled "Hey! What are you kids doin' on my property?"

His quick response to this capitalist (as Debussy calls anyone who places such importance in private property) was "Unless you plan on giving us a ride home or gettin' rid of that stupid skateboarding law, we'll just have to keep takin' the shortcut. The closest distance between two points is a straight line; not our fault you had to position your stupid house in the straight line between our homes and school. Us students are claimin' eminent domain on this wall, which is in the way of our direct path home."

Debussy and Christopher were surprised Nathan remembered anything from geometry.

Angrily the man replied, "If I see you on my wall again, I'm gonna have to call the police!"

"Instead of gawking like a head with your chicken cut off, why don't you get your ugly ass up here and do somethin' about it?" Nathan spit back at him.

With that final gesture of contempt for the homeowner, Christopher and Debussy picked up their pace to a jog. Nathan, however, knew the old man couldn't get one foot on the wall. Being about as big as the old fart, Nathan fearlessly sauntered on, not letting the man's grumbles phase him in the least.

Today hopefully no one would intrude on their journey. As they made jokes about each other, Debussy suddenly stopped short in his tracks. "You guys ssshhhh! Look! Look at that beauty!" Debussy pointed with one hand, the other to his lips.

"We've struck gold baby!" Christopher whispered excitedly.

Debussy and Christopher were more excited about the adventure of discovery and confiscation than they were about the rewarded treasure they received at the end of their journey. Debussy thought of how Alexander "the Great" would give away all his treasures to his army after a war and declare "All I need as rewards are my hopes and dreams."

It was the chase, not the catch that inspired these adventures. However, as long as Nathan would receive the final glory of the catch, he assumed leave the chase to Christopher, Debussy, and anyone else he could convince to do the dirty work. Needless to say, they made a perfect team.

"What I don't see it?" Nathan grumbled.

"Ssshhh, you're gonna blow it, dude!"

Nestled tightly between a tool shed and a fence wound with tomato vines-a perfect camouflage for anyone entering the yard from the sliding glass door of the house-sprouted a healthy bush, with long buds, dripping with resin. "Damn would you look at the size of those buds!?!" Christopher said in a soft, excited whisper, almost hyperventilating.

Nathan finally caught sight of it. "Fuck! Party!"

"O.K.; Chris you take the front. I'll take the back. And Nate, you cover." Debussy strategized quickly. They had the art down to a tee.

Nathan broke in, "Wait, that's one damn big weed. It's gonna be a bitch pullin' up. It'll take a heavyweight. Remember last time?"

***

Who could forget last time; it took two to pull up the plant, leaving Christopher with no back up, and they almost got caught. They had quite a routine, but on occasion, not all went as planned. Luckily Debussy's brother, Zeus had a paper route, so they were accustomed to soliciting door to door for new customers. They had their alibi all worked out. One of them would go to the front door, knock, and pretend to be soliciting for the paper. If no one answered, he would whistle to his back up, who stayed on the side of the house keeping guard. The back up would then whistle to the one in the rear, who would jump into the backyard, grab the plant, scale the wall, then finally whistle to the back up and solicitor, letting all know the deed was done.

***

Debussy finally decided, with the help of Nathan's persuasion, he'd go to the front door. Christopher reluctantly would stand cover, while Nathan would fetch the plant-this time actually doing a little work for the glory. All took their places, as Debussy knocked on the door with his heart in his mouth, each second nervously expecting someone to answer. After a minute or so, he tried once more, just to be double safe. When no one answered the second time, he whistled to Christopher, who volleyed back to Nathan.

Nathan breathed in deeply, touched his head, chest, then his shoulders-jokingly to Christopher, who still believed in that superstitious stuff-the Father, Son, and so on. He loved making fun of it. After another breath he jumped down. "Oh! Damn!" He landed and fell to his side, as his ankle gave way.

"Ssshhh!" Protested Christopher. "We're gonna get caught." Christopher was always pretending bravery before hand, and today was no exception. He started breathing heavily, afraid someone might have heard Nathan's fall. He looked around nervously. After a moment's pause, Nathan stood up and brushed the dirt off his knees. With a slight limp, he jogged over to grab his prize. He pulled with all his strength, making a grunting sound, and then repeated attempts caused him to fall back on the ground.

Meanwhile, Debussy, noticing a car pulling around the corner, heading straight for the house, became nervous. His breath grew heavy. As if in freeze-frame, he could see the car signal and turn up the driveway. Under his breath he sighed, "Fuck!" He had no time to signal to Christopher. Suddenly he was at a loss of what to say. As he tried to collect his thoughts, the car door opened. As if in slow mode, a well-dressed man, with arms full of groceries stepped out, wearing an irritated look on his face, which seemed to say, "Get lost kid. I've had a long day!"

Debussy, now shaking slightly, gulped and gave the following delivery. "Ah. Hi sir. I'm ah," He couldn't for the first time, as if this unwanted visitor had stolen the words form his memory, remember his lines. "Well, I'm selling papers." Following this with a half self-deprecating smile.

He was trained to never say those last two words. His normal spiel was: "I'm involved in the Wutherington Post's After-School Youth Program, 'Save-a-Teen.' We're helping keep kids out of gangs. (As if there were any gangs in this suburban paradise.) We're giving neighbors a special chance to start up a one-year subscription at a reduced price, at the same time helping to 'save a teen.' You see, the first month's cost will go straight to the 'save-a-teen' foundation."

Debussy didn't really believe any of this money would actually be used for its supposed purpose. He rarely trusted the legitimacy of any organization, and he had much less faith in capitalist institutions, whose main purposes was to reap a profit, but knowing they were using him, he felt it was his duty to use them back with a vengeance. Not only did he make money for munchies; he also stood to get a weekly trip to Punchy's Pizza and Arcade, if he got two new customers. He would also be rewarded with five dollars in tokens, to entertain his addiction to video games. However, as he missed every line of his well-rehearsed speech, his solicitee remarked, "I have no time for papers!"

Fighting his nervous convulsions, Debussy struggled to buy time, by rebutting the man's objection. "Well you see, ah, sir, you can be helping our, ah, youth program." And then gritting his teeth at his terrible rebuttal, he tried to catch the fumble, but again sapient words wouldn't come.

Meanwhile Nathan, still struggling in the backyard, gave up on pulling the plant out with his hands. Instead, he proceeded to kick the bottom of its trunk, to break it off. This only further aggravated his twisted ankle. Eventually, he managed to split the trunk, and twisting it in circles, finally broke it off-but at the expense of smashing a few large, low hanging buds, which remained scattered on the ground. Limping, he carried his prize, with sweat on his brow and a full smile on his face, unconscious of Debussy's struggle in the front. "Shit look at this. Ha ha!"

"shh!" Whispered Christopher. "You're gonna fuckin' blow it!"

As he handed the plant up to Christopher, they heard the front door slam, which prompted Christopher to shove the plant in the bag and run along the wall as far away from the house as possible, leaving Nathan helplessly trying to scale the wall alone with his hurt foot. Then when Nathan heard the back door being unlocked, he gave up on the climb, and jumped between the tool shed and the brick wall. He laid there amongst cobwebs, trembling, with his face planted, kissing the dirt, holding his breath, hoping he wouldn't get caught.

The man grabbed his garden hose and was preparing to water his plant, when to his surprise he noticed his purple-hared Sinsemilla had been replaced with a mound of dirt and some scattered leaves. He screamed out at the top of his lungs, "God, mother-fuckin' damn!" He followed the track of dirt to the wall, where he could see Christopher running on the wall, about five houses down, with the bag spilling dirt out the top. The man knew he wouldn't catch him on foot, so he ran through the house, jumped into his car, and peeled out of the driveway, leaving the back and front doors wide open.

As Nathan heard the tires squeal away, he got up, wiped the cobwebs from his hair, brushed the dirt from his clothes, and made a quick break, limping through the house. He stopped half way through to swipe some adult magazines off the bookshelf as souvenirs. Then out the front door he ran, the opposite way of the car, through the neighborhood.

Christopher, knowing the man might try to head him off at the end of the row of houses, made the most of his athletic abilities. He jumped into one of the yards and climbed over a fence that led through an industrial area, then ran through some oil fields, and quickly lost the unfortunate old man.

Going Underground

Hidden Valley was one of the few remaining areas where kids could hide away from the growing suburbs. It was rare to see an adult in this valley. Its two beautiful ponds-full of crawdads, frogs and polliwogs-were hidden by a canopy of tall trees. The banks of these ponds offered a cool place to play. The neighborhood kids tied ropes from trees, and would swing down the surrounding hillsides and plunge into the cool water. The hills were carved into bicycle tracks and jumps.

Though they all went their separate ways, eventually the three met at the top of the valley's hills, in their underground clubhouse. The clubhouse was built in the center of the grassy plain, which surrounded the perimeter of the valley. It was four feet deep and six feet, by eight feet wide. They carpeted it with large pieces of discarded rug, which they found behind a building supply and home improvement store. They dug seats in the walls. Over the carpet, which lined the seats, they placed cushions from abandoned couches. Two by four boards were placed over the dugout and topped with plywood. Dirt was pored over the plywood, then grass, bushes and tumbleweed over the dirt, which camouflaged it as part of the field. The hideout had a small hatch doorway on the side, which when opened, led down a few steps. Adorning the walls were candle holders and fliers from their favorite local punk band concerts: *The Circle Jerks*, *The Dead Kennedys*, *Social Distortion*, *Wasted Youth*, *Suicidal Tendencies*, *Great Britain Hate*-names that caused adults to sneer in consternation.

Draped form the ceiling of this hobble of escape, was an American flag-the all mighty "bars and stars," with big burn holes and tare holes, which they added to each day. It was their act of celebration for their freedom from authority, which they enjoyed fully here.

No teachers. No cops. No parents!

They could hide away for hours, not having to worry about anyone telling them: "You can't do this," or "You can't do that"-which was exactly why they did everything they did, because people told them they couldn't.

It was a great bastion for open thought and open expression. They could sing out loudly the lyrics of their favorite punk songs:

"Anarchy Burger,
Hold the government!"

Christopher got there first; for he never looked back and kept running. When Nathan and Debussy arrived, Christopher was lying on his back in the middle of the fort, with his prized bag on his chest. It heaved up and down, even though he had plenty of time to catch his breath, by the time the other two had arrived. His heart wouldn't stop pounding. Sweat dripped down the sides of his face.

Although it was hot outside, the insulation of mud and clay kept the fort pleasantly cool. Walking down the steps they both laughed at their scared sick friend prostrate on the floor. "You make the best fuckin' jack rabbit I've ever seen." Nathan smirked, as Debussy laughed along. "The blood hounds would never catch your ugly ass. Ha ha!"

Christopher didn't laugh back. He just kept panting heavily and stared with dazed eyes at the torn flag hanging above his head. Two burn holes like eyes seem to stare back at him. He felt his whole country was looking down on him. When he was forced to do that daily "pledge" in school, he would shake in his shoes, thinking he was being a bad "patriot." The religion of Nationalism had an even stronger control of him, than did that botched Roman one.

***

When Christopher moved to this town two years prior, he was a straight A student, though more by force than will. He never in his wildest dreams would have thought of stealing anything, nor would he have known how. But boy did he learn a thing or two from Nathan and Debussy.

At the time of his arrival to Wutherington Beach, Nathan was the most popular kid in the seventh grade. He was the class clown, whom everyone wanted to hang around on lunch breaks. When Christopher first entered Bellevue Middle School, he was petrified by the large hallways and the towering stairways, which led up to this colossal edifice. To him, although he had never been to the District of Columbia, the school resembled the US Capitol building, with great chandelier laden cathedral ceilings and mammoth arched walkways. It had no resemblance to the little schoolhouse he left behind in that small town of Palookaville, Nebraska.

As he walked down those hallways two years ago, he passed Nathan, who sat just outside the doors of his forth-period reading class. The teacher was punishing him for talking too much while the others tried to read. It seemed to most that he spent more time in detention than in class.

Nathan had to say something to everyone walking by. So he said to this strange new kid, "What you can't find your way to the potty? It's that way." Christopher knew this guy was only trying to agitate him. So he walked on nervously, not saying a word.

"What a cat got your tongue?" Nathan giggled, although not following it with the normal belly rolling sound, which he was so infamous for.

As he watched the kid turn the corner, for once in his life, showing some sense of humanity, he actually felt a little sorry for this new kid. He couldn't understand why. As if he had some connection with this stranger, he felt that as the boy turned the corner, for a brief moment he was walking in the kid's shoes. He had seen those "new age" shows on "out of body experiences" and the like. He never quite understood what they were, but he thought to himself, "Maybe that's what they meant on TV?"

Whatever it was, from that day forward Nathan decided he would show this kid the ropes around school. And although he loved picking on him, next to Debussy of course, he considered Christopher his best friend.

***

As Christopher lay there staring at the flag his mind dwelled on how fast those two years flew by, and how they drastically changed his perception of reality. During the previous twelve years in Nebraska, he never would have imagined smoking pot. He couldn't even imagine smoking a cigarette. Now there seemed very little he hadn't tried. He couldn't fathom ever being more experienced in life than he was now.

Nathan sat in his throne. He lit the candle closest him, then snagged the bag from Christopher's chest. He pulled out a long dripping bud, put it to his nose, and with a smile on his face, inhaled the sweet smell of Sinsemilla. "Ahh! Yeah! Now that's Heaven!"

"Give me a whiff of that shit." Debussy grabbed a handful of the vine. With an exhilarating breath, which seemed to last an eternity he exclaimed, "Aahhh....."

Christopher finally coming to his senses let out a long breath. "Sswwoo..."

"You got the pipe Chris?" Nathan rummaged through his bag.

"No but I brought an aluminum can. Remember Zeus borrowed the pipe last night?" It wasn't much of a pipe anyway. It was the end attachment of a water faucet turned upside down. They covered the bowl with a lint screen. Turning the handle of the faucet made a perfect carburetor. Although the can worked just as well.

Nathan always had a few safety pins holding up the cuffs of his jeans. He pulled one out and handed it to Debussy. Debussy flattened the side of the can and proceeded to poke holes in a circular pattern on the flattened side, until it made a nice pipe screen. Then jabbing a key in the back end for a carburetor, now their pipe was ready to go.

Once they were in their safety zone, they didn't once bring up the earlier fiasco, as if it were an everyday occurrence. They didn't consider it "cool" to make a stink over a little dramatic moment. They acted like close calls were part of their daily routine. Now their minds were absorbed in completely letting go-putting everything behind them-slipping totally into fantasy-letting all memories of Mr. Cranston's first day's homework assignment be totally forgotten. Of course Christopher couldn't let go or forget everything, completely.

But the other two tried.

They never had the patience to dry out their bud. After Debussy crafted his pipe, Nathan handed him his lighter and a large bud, which was about one inch in diameter. It was a deep forest green, adorned with burgundy-brown cilia like hairs peeking out of it. Debussy stuck it over the circular holed pattern, holding the can sideways with the top opening to his lips. And with the index finger of the hand holding the can, he covered the carburetor. With his diaphragm taut, he pushed out all the air in his body to enjoy the fullest inhalation of this "sacred Mary Jane."

As the flint of the lighter sparked, he squinted his eyes in ecstasy, as if preparing to kiss a beautiful girl. Sucking the flame over the pipe, he proceeded to pull it down through the bud. With a "snap, crackly, popping" sound, the bud glowed reddish orange. With his chest protruding, he filled his upper body with the soft herbal fumes they so loved. Suddenly, a warmth enveloped him. He could feel it spread down his back, through his tired legs, and tingle in his toes. The soreness he bore from the run slowly evaporated into the cool air. When his lungs were replete, he expanded his diaphragm to pull the smoke down further into the lower recesses of his wind chamber.

Nathan now watery eyed and drooling, stared with restless excitement, and finally broke the silence. "OK already. Don't fuckin' Bogart it now!"

Grunting like a pig through his nose, Debussy handed the can to his friend, who seized it as a child would snatch a cookie from his mother's cookie jar, and feverishly lit the lighter. Debussy held his breath, bobbing up and down with elation, for as long as he could. He queezed inaudibly some popular saying (who knows or cares what). Nathan knew the feeling was beyond words and fully understood Debussy's sentiment. As he held his breath, he could hear his heart beat like a tribal drone that echoed in his head. He felt a sense of weightlessness, as he floated in his chair. The hair on the back of his neck, meanwhile, stood erect. Then finally cracking his lips, he slowly pushed out a billowing cloud of smoke in the direction of Christopher's face, who was still laid out on the floor, though slightly awake now.

Christopher finally smelling the vapor, stirred to his feet, and took his place on his padded chair. He wiped his eyes sleepily and yawned fakingly. He pretended often he was too tired to smoke out. But in fact, he was too scared. He wanted to be accepted in the group, so reluctantly he did as they did. However, he tried, though seldom succeeded, in getting out of it, for fear his parents would find out. When Nathan was finished with his hit, he passed it to Christopher. But Christopher retorted, "Ah, I'm too tired. I'll get all burnt out."

"Stop trying to puss out on us. Fuckin' wimp; take a hit!" Nathan stuck it in his face. So Christopher reluctantly took it, lit it up, and playing Bill Clinton, barely inhaled.

"Shit, what are you thinking? Give it to Debussy if you're gonna be such a sissy!" Nathan ripped it from his hand, causing the bud to drop to the carpet.

Christopher blew out the little smoke he had taken in. "What are you talkin' about? I took as much as I could." He objected, in a whinny voice.

"Yeah! As much as my cat, Momma Sita can handle. Look! Now you fuckin' dropped it all over the place." Nathan socked Christopher on the arm.

"OK. Chill man. We got a whole stinkin' bag here." Debussy interrupted, trying to pacify his agitated friend.

"Yeah! Tha's easy for *you* to say. *You* didn't fuckin' practically brake *your* damn leg, and risk *your* damn life back there. And *Christopher* goes and runs off like a damn cheetah, and leaves *us* to get caught, while *he's* back here resting, and then pussin' out, saying *he's* too tired to smoke out, as if *he* did any work." Nathan went on and on to make Christopher feel guilty if he didn't get stoned with them. He was a pro at that kind of manipulation.

Christopher, with tears almost coming to his eyes, interrupted. "OK! O fuckin' K, already! Fuckin' give me the damn pipe you jack ass!" He picked it up and took some more from the bag, and lit it up-this time taking a real hit.

Nathan screamed out excitedly. "That's it! That's it! Now hold it in! Hold it fuckin' in! Yeah! Now that's it!"

As Christopher was turning blue from lack of oxygen, Nathan socked him in the stomach, only hard enough to make him cough up the smoke. Nathan and Debussy busted out laughing at the top of their lungs. Christopher, feeling a little light headed, finally joined in. They did a couple more rounds. Nathan remembered he had swiped the adult magazines from their victim, so he pulled them out, and they all looked through them and laughed.

And as they were giggling hysterically, Nathan said to Christopher "Hey was it on the 'fifth day' or the 'sixth day' that God made Mary Jane?"

Christopher was the only one in the group who still had a belief in a "God." Or actually, it was more a fear than a belief. He was afraid if there was a God, he would be damned on "Judgment Day." This fear had almost as much control over his actions, as did his parent's dreaded retaliation for his misdeeds. These two fears combined placed such a heavy toll on his consciousness that he had to occasionally get a little sedated just to be able to breathe normally. They caused such a strangle hold on his life-force that his health began to suffer. He was always getting sick. And he suffered from the common "mother love" asthma, kids with overbearing mothers often suffer. Luckily, Nathan and Debussy had acquired much healthier philosophies to live by. Nathan, born to two parents from Northern Ireland, knew all too well the folly of religious dogma, and how destructive religious fanaticism can be. His mother, Christina Phelps was a recovering Catholic. His father, Richard Phelps was an "awoke again" atheist, once under the spell of Protestantism. They left their barbaric war torn families behind, going against their wishes not to marry. He loved to poke fun at Christopher's professed beliefs, and was amused by Christopher's lack of historical understanding of those beliefs. Like many so-called "Christians," his faith was just a formality, lacking any real grounding in everyday life.

Debussy, who thought the idea of anyone still believing in "that superstitious crap," as he called it, was utterly absurd. Laughingly, he joined in his favorite discussion. “Yeah! And on the ‘eighth day’ he was sucking on Lori Thompson’s tits!” Nathan and Debussy started rolling on the floor, laughing till their cheeks hurt and their sides ached.

Debussy

Debussy was born into a very freethinking family. His late father, Charles Xanthankis, a writer, poet, and musician named him after his favorite composer of avant-garde music. He had the nurse of the hospital Debussy was born in grudgingly type in the column of his birth certificate that specified his religion "All or None!" Debussy's mother and father were very progressive. He adopted their philosophy, which included questioning all beliefs and ideologies. It emphasized learning to think for yourself.

While his mother, Justine Jensen ("J.J." as everyone called her) was away at work, he loved to browse through the scientific journals that decorated her coffee table. He learned from them that the visible ends of the universe were now believed to be somewhere between fifteen to seventeen billion light years away. He couldn't see how any modern thinker, armed with the latest scientific information, could logically fit some creator or that old "Heavenly Jerusalem" world-view into this new scientific equation, without completely ignoring it.

Debussy's father died when he was two years old. His older Brother, Zeus was almost four at the time. (Justine came up with Zeus's name from the Greek Mythology class she was taking in high school, when she got pregnant with him in her senior year.) Although the kids were too young to really understand why or how their father died, and the mystery that stayed in their minds was kept to themselves, they loved to amuse their friends with fantastic and heroic stories. Out of fear, however, mostly of their mother's reaction, over those preceding twelve or so years they never questioned her about his death. Equally mysterious to them was the reason their last name had been changed from the unusual Greek name Xanthankis, to a common name like Jensen-for which there were no other relatives on either side of the family sharing this new name. But the years simply passed by, and they never got around to asking her why.

The two brothers shared a mixed heritage of Greek, Italian, German, Irish, and American-Seminole Indian. The Native American side was from their father's grandmother. After their father died, his side of the family from back east lost touch with them, probably in part because of the sudden name change. However, Debussy, although only one 5th Native American held the most pride in that ancestry. He would often say he was half Native American and half "European Mutt." He would also say, "We are all born part angel and part devil, though we must learn to keep the angel in control of the devil."

Since his mother worked two or three odd jobs at a time (As a hairdresser, a waitress, and a jewelry store clerk) the two boys mostly raised themselves. Although there were ever-changing babysitters, mostly Spanish speaking, who offered to watch them for next to nothing, these babysitters usually had many kids of their own and couldn't give Debussy or Zeus that much individual attention. In addition, with the language barrier between them and their sitters, it was each brother relying on the other for advice and encouragement that got them through those early days of youth. Although Debussy looked up to Zeus, in many ways he felt he should have been born as the older brother. Perhaps he believed he had been in a previous life. Although Zeus was more organized with his physical possessions, Debussy felt a much greater control of his emotions, and seemed to have more direction in life. The former was more left-brain and anal retentive, while the latter was much more creative, intuitive, and clearly, dominantly right brain.

It was in this freethinking environment that Debussy adopted a dislike for anything dogmatic or authoritarian. He had an avid thirst for knowledge and an interest in any information that went against the mainstream glut, of what he would say was "misinformation fed to me at this white majority, 'conservative' institution." The "institution" he referred to was obviously the school system that to him didn't allow people to really grow into independent, thinking people. He felt the capitalistic educational system, and its huge corporate owned textbook manufacturers led people to become nothing but hard working corporate puppets, and acquiescent mindless "consumers." He resented and refused to take part with such socialization, as being forced to take part in the daily solute to the "Bars and Stars." He also had a predilection for reading that which was controversial or which caused him to stretch his mind beyond the plebeian concerns of his insular and extremely myopic community.

Debussy's mother supported his independent state-of-mind. One time he was called into the vice-principal's office because he was the first boy at the school to pierce his ear. When Debussy refused to take out his earring, the vice-principal called in Justine for a parent's conference. However, this proved fruitless, when Justine threatened to file charges of sexual discrimination. Her argument was: if girls were allowed to wear earrings at the school, there's no reason why boys shouldn't be able to. Although Justine was supportive of Debussy's freethinking, due to the hardship of single parenting she had over the years slowly lost her own active zest for learning and revolutionary thinking. She had outgrown her belief that she could change the world, but luckily, Debussy was far more idealistic.

The Discovery

Last summer Debussy made a discovery, which would continue forever altering his perception of reality. It was a warm July weekday afternoon. He and Nathan were trying to find a hiding place to stash some weed they'd seized from a downtown neighbor's backyard.

His mother's garage was kept locked at all times. It was used only to store boxes of various nick-knacks, which were leftovers from their move into their small apartment, shortly after Mr. Xanthankis's death. Without her husband's small income, Justine had to move the kids into this rundown, cramped up apartment and store away most of their belongings, until someday, when she hoped to move the family into a more spacious home. But now, it was twelve years later and that day still hadn't come.

This apartment complex they lived in (occupied by mostly Spanish speaking, migrant workers and their families) was situated on the outskirts of downtown, in an area many of the more affluent residents snobbishly referred to as "the projects." Of course every middle-class beach community had to have a place where the cities trash truck drivers, gardeners, and widowed parents could live. And "Delaware Manor" was just the place.

The apartment Debussy's family shared was right above the garage units. The garages were separated by a thin wooden wall about six and a half feet tall, leaving an opening about two feet wide at the ceiling. The neighbor who shared the garage next door used his only to park his car and often left it wide open. At times he pulled the car out into the driveway, and could usually be found under the hood, doing regular maintenance on his jalopy.

Debussy rarely conversed with his neighbors. It wasn't that he didn't want to; it was their lack of ability in the English language, which made any meaningful communication impossible. However, at times he would try to throw out the few Spanish words, which he had learned from his babysitter's kids. Everyone was amused by his bad pronunciation.

That afternoon his next-door neighbor left his garage door open all day. Debussy and Nathan climbed the dividing walls of the garage and went to hide their goods in one of the boxes that filled the garage.

"Hey Nathan. Shit. Give me your lighter. I can't see crap." Debussy called out in the dark, trying not to trip over all the junk. "Ah! Ah damn!" He shouted, as he fell over a stack of magazines.

"What? You need some fuckin' training wheels to keep yourself up?" Nathan laughed. They lit the candles, which they kept in their stash bag.

The garage was littered with cobwebs, dust, and boxes-hidden memories of the life Justine once shared with Charles. Nathan started opening boxes. "Books… Full… Ah, more books… Full… Shit how many fuckin' books you guys got in here? You didn't tell me your father ran a damn library."

"Let me see!" Debussy moved over to the candlelight with excitement, and started sorting through them. "Ah, *CIA and the Cult of Intelligence. Hemp: Lifeline to the Future. Unlocking the Mysteries of Birth and Death.* Man these books are punk! *Make-Believe Media.*" He read the titles out loud as he flipped through the books, with intoxication.

Getting annoyed, Nathan grabbed the candle and yelled out "What, did we climb in here to fuckin' study in the dark; or are we gonna find a place to stash our bud before your mom comes home?"

"Come on; I just want to check out a few of these!"

"Your mom's gonna be home soon. We better hurry and hide this shit." Nathan finally found a box that contained only a few antiques. He stuck the bag inside.

"Dude just pour it in the box. I'm gonna put some of these books in that bag."

"OK, it's gonna be your bust, when your mom finds pieces of leaf all over the bottom of the box."

"My mom hasn't fuckin' opened the damn garage for over a decade." At this point, Debussy didn't care much about the pot or hiding it. The boxes of books and their strange titles made his curiosity peak to the height of enthusiasm. He felt a sense of nostalgia, imagining these were the same books his father read-the dad whom the only memory he still recalled of was that big bag of cookies he left on the counter the day before the last trip of his life to Central America.

Debussy crammed as many books as he could carry without ripping open the bag. From that day on, for the rest of the summer, Debussy would hide himself away somewhere, and veraciously eat away at the contents of these secret books. He kept the bag under his bed, safely tucked behind shoe boxes, so his mom wouldn't notice he had them-afraid she might keep them from him, had she have known.

Anyone would probably keep them from him, if they only knew the secrets they revealed-secrets that demolished those lies he'd been force fed by his barbarous culture-the propaganda that had been sold to him by corporate America-the lame excuses for "news," which he had been a victim of ever since he first learned to suck the "boob tube." Every myth from "milk it does a body good" to "USA's keeping the world safe for democracy" was slowly dispelled like ranking armpit odor being blown out by one refreshing spray of deodorant. Finally he had verifiable reason to distrust the mainstream, right-wing, "conservative" brainwashing, crap he already so despised.

He always hated TV commercialism, and refused to be caught dead wearing their "just do it" child, slave-labor made tennis shoes. He felt like busting the TV screen whenever he saw that despicable excuse of a public servant, Newt Gin"Grinch" talk out his ass about his "Contract Against Americans." He knew no corporate puppet head in Washington gave a damn about his mother working three jobs to keep the family alive- be them "Demican," "Republicrat," or one of those cross breed "Demo-Republicrats," like Billy, "ah, I didn't inhale," Clinton. He believed, as Marx wrote, that the government in a capitalist system is simply the administrative arm of the rich, upper class, bourgeoisie. He must had somehow inherited a small gene of progressive intelligence from his father, which helped him intuitively discern between reality and the utter nonsense he was daily bombarded with in this fairy tail land of "Califia."

These books contained the revolutionary political writings of such great minds as Dr. Michael Parenti, Gore Vidal, Professor Noam Chomsky, Helen Caldicott-just to name a few. He dabbled in writings of historians like Toynbee, Sorokin, Spengler, and Quigley, and found magazines like "The Nation," "The Progressive," and "Mother Jones"-fabulous muck racking journals, all of which added insight to the works of these great revolutionaries. He read biographies and autobiographies of such heroes of humanity as Steven Biko, Che Guevara, Jose Marti, and Martin Luther King Jr.-men who risked their lives to stand up for truth and justice in a world where it was so lacking.

He read things that although they disgusted him, didn't totally surprise him. After all, one of his slogans was "I love my country. But I can't trust my government." He read from Mortimer Adler what he had always expected-that his government was never founded as a "democracy," and was never intended to represent one either. As Mortimer wrote, "The notion that this country was founded as a democracy, of course, is sheer rot. It was anything but that." He learned that it was started as the greatest oligarchy ever, as Mortimer stated "an oligarchy of the most severe kind." Through these great books, he learned about how corrupt the CIA is, and how their initials could be more truly interpreted as the "Capitalist International Army" or perhaps the "Cocaine Import Agency." Since true "Intelligence" was something they completely lack. It was no wonder to him why both the Kennedy brothers had been taken out, especially when both tried to limit the power of that evil, intelligence/terrorist organization.

He learned about their nefarious dealings in Central, and South America, Asia and Africa. He read how, with US taxpayers' money, death squads in all the countries of those continents were trained and covertly financed by this agency and other crooked arms of the state department, like the DOD, and DEA, through the "black budget"-that budget that not even congress was allowed to review, lest they be killed like the Kennedys. It involved drug dealing and other criminal acts to raise money for covert operations that no civil person would possibly approve. All in the interest of preventing democratic change, which might upset US and Western capital penetration and exploitation into these "mal-developed" and "over-exploited" countries, as Dr. Parenti called them.

He also discovered how most, if not all, of the leaders of these death squads, and the military leaders and presidents of the countries that employed them, were often trained by the US, often on US soil, in such infantry schools as "The School of the Americas" in Fort Benning, Georgia. This school was dubbed by many humanitarian organizations in Latin America: "The School of The Assassins"-where decorated graduates became leaders of such criminal organizations as "The Contras"-that drug dealing, Mafioso style organization that was funded by CIA drug money and trained by the CIA and other infamous parts of the so-called US "Defense Department." He learned that ruthless military dictators, such as Manuel Noriega of Panama and Hugo Banzer of Bolivia, were among the school's "Hall of Fame"-or as Senator Edward Kennedy called it, the "Hall of Shame."

He read how colonialism never really ended as his apologetic, revisionist history books tried to falsely portray it-as if it was some relic of some "past" America. These books taught him that it was just converted to a less costly form of what could be termed "corporate colonialism." Big transnational "American" corporations, once they grew larger than the national government, and once they completely infiltrated the American and other so-called "first world" governments, found it much more profitable to extend their dominion by getting in bed with smaller government's oligarchs. And when sex with these governments wasn't submitted to, rape would follow.

This prevented the corporations from being held accountable for any liability if their callous business dealings caused destruction or waste. The responsibility for cleaning up was dumped on the citizens of the nations, who were exploited at the hands of these rip-off artists. This practice was neatly referred to by economist as "externalizing cost" and "internalizing profits"-part of the master plans of such notorious WTO trade "agreements" like NAFTA and GATT, and financed by such undemocratic, elitist organizations, as the World Bank and the IMF. The corporations get the rewards, the citizens foot the bill, and the oligarch are fed handsomely by corporate kickbacks to subjugate their meek populations and to keep them meek.

If these governments didn't sell off the people's lands or support the huge corporations' deceitful dealings, the "Capitalist International Army (CIA)" would help install a more "corporate friendly" government, like the murderous Indonesian, Iraqi, or Chilean governments, which the US helped prop up. However, they often had to destroy those governments and the people in those countries once they no longer acquiesced and did their bidding. Iraq was a classic example of such a change of heart by the US State Department. These governments, with their ruthless police and military forces, would uproot people, who once live off the lands, and then they would sell great tracks of land to huge American and European agribusiness plantations and factories at garage sale prices. Of course these businesses were more than happy to employ the displaced and starving populace at practically slave wages. This helped cause much of the people in Central and South America, and other Asian, Middle Eastern, and African countries to live far below the poverty line.

The books being his father's were all at least a decade old. He wondered if this disruptive corporate behavior persisted until today. If so, why had he never heard any word of it in his school history books or in the mainstream media? This curiosity brought him on a journey to the Wutherington Beach Public Library- a beautiful four-story glass building in the middle of Central Park.

He walked down the stone spiraling walkway, which circled a flowing fountain. It led him to the bottom floor where the therapeutic sounds of running water enveloped him. He got on one of the computer catalogs and searched a subject, which he thought must be in this giant edifice-"controversial history." Under that heading he found a very interesting book: *Lies My Teacher Told me; Everything American History Books Got Wrong.* He then searched under the heading- "corporate abuse." There he found *When Corporations Rule the World.* Finally under "corruption in politics," he found, *Washington on Ten Million Dollar A Day*, and *Senator For Sale,* a brilliant expose' on Mr. Personality himself, Bob Dole.

Then he started to search for books by his favorite author in his father's collection, Michael Parenti. Under that author, he found an incredible book about American capitalist exploitation around the world, *Against Empire*. He also found *The Sword and The Dollar*, and *Inventing Reality*, a book about corruption in the US mainstream media.

He sat back in a chair as the sound of water cleansed him of societies hypnotizing myths. He inhaled the contents of these books, until he found some sense of clarity to his questioning. He was able to discover the reasons his history books and the corporate owned media overlooked or purposely avoided much of America's unsavory history. To admit the past would be to admit the present, which is an ongoing extension of that hidden and forgotten past. He found that the so-called "democracy" in America was really plutocracy-a land ruled by money and greed, or perhaps a kleptocracy, ruled by criminals. Those with the money fiercely tried to keep the general public ignorant of how they had obtained such wealth, by the blood, sweat and toil of million of used and abused human beings.

Up into the Sun

After a few hours in the hole, Nathan, Debussy and Christopher crawled up out of their smoke filled den, eyes blazing red, stomachs growling and laughing up a storm. They squinted as the sun blazed down upon them. As Christopher poked his head up through the doorway, Nathan had a perfect opportunity to limpy him right on the forehead.

"Fuckin' cock sucker!"

"Ha ha! Shut up you wimp."

Debussy protecting his underdog friend Charley-horsed Nathan and ran off busting up. Nathan still limping slightly tried to catch up with Debussy. But he lagged far behind. Then Christopher ran after both of them. As he caught up with Nathan, he prepared his limp ring finger for a sure shot at Nathan's cerebellum. He gave him a good whack, circled him, avoiding his swinging arms. And chuckling, he easily passed him up.

"You damn jack ass!"

"Yeah, eat me."

Christopher finally came abreast with Debussy. They gave each other high fives, then climbed the brick wall that demarcated the boundaries of Hidden Valley and the new jumbo strip mall. They were right behind the neighborhood's new super-store, a big-time local grocery megatropolis.

***

This new giant grocery store, which was smartly called "The Big Store," was built after the owning company's hostile corporate takeover of a competing chain of stores. The two previous companies had smaller markets, each on opposite sides of town. The new corporation opened this mega-store in the center of town, shortly before it closed their two smaller markets. Not only was this jumbo-store super-big, but it was also mega-crowded and sported outrageously long lines and highly inflated prices.

Although it was twice the size of its predecessors, it employed far fewer people. Its zealous board of directors was sure the store could manage well with less of their middle management, and without many of their higher salaried employees. (Though they had never worked in stores themselves and probably rarely shopped for themselves-like George Bush Sr., they probably had never even seen those electronic scanners at a grocery line.) Experts at downsizing, they laid off a third of their previous employees. They knew the cost cuts would please their greedy stockholders. And for their reckless behavior they were rewarded handsomely with stock options and other undeserved benefits.

With less competition the citizens of Wutherington Beach had to eat the higher prices and bare the longer lines. With less supervision and a far less knowledgeable service staff the store became quite chaotic. However it was a welcome change for Nathan, Debussy and Christopher. They found this mega-store much better suited for shoplifting. They didn't miss the smaller, more organized markets one bit.

***

Debussy and Christopher sat on the wall snickering as Nathan came staggering and gasping for air to the bottom of the wall. He tried to jump up and grab onto the ledge. However, he slid right back down. "Fuckin' one of you guys help me up?"

"All right, say you're sorry and I'll help you up." Christopher bargained.

"Ah, OK. I'm, ah, sorry you're a dick head."

"Fine, stay down there. We'll just have to have a picnic without you."

"Come on Debut? Help me up?"

After laughing awhile, Debussy felt a little sorry for his friend. He finally jumped down to give Nathan a hand. Nathan stepped on Debussy's locked hands, reached one arm over the wall and pulled his body halfway up. Laughing, Nathan kicked Debussy's head with his other foot, causing Debussy to fall back on the dirt. Nathan scrambled to get up the wall before Debussy could catch him. But the latter was far too quick. He jumped up and tugged on Nathan's sore leg, bringing him down right on top of Debussy's side.

Christopher busted up hysterically as Nathan got Debussy in a headlock and started noogying him. They both rolled in the dirt. Christopher finally joined in the excitement. He scaled halfway down the wall and in midair performed a perfect cannonball onto the center of Nathan's back, knocking him right off of Debussy.

This time Christopher and Debussy were able to dog pile atop Nathan, who was way too exhausted to resist. After a minute or so they all got worn-out and stopped wrestling. They laid back on the ground staring at the setting sun, as its fingers poked through the distant trees. Although they were sore and bruised they were too sedated to be mad at each other. They just kept laughing until their cheeks could no longer hold their grins.

"Fuck, that was some good ass bud, Debut." Nathan smiled in delight.

"Ha, ha, yeah."

"Shit, my mom's gonna kill me when she sees my clothes." Christopher chuckled, finally too stoned to give a damn.

After a while they stumbled to their feet. Both Debussy and Christopher finally helped Nathan up the wall-but only after repeated promises he would do no more tricks.

Picnic Time

The three boys paraded through an exiting crowd of people, who were hurrying to get home to cook up dinner for their families. Debussy whispered to Christopher "Hey, go grab us some eye drops from the medicine area, so people won't notice our eyes."

Ignoring his request he said, "Shit, I'm getting me some cup cakes."

As they skipped down the candy isle, Nathan picked up a candy bar, looked around to make sure no one saw and then hurled it at the back of Christopher's head. "Fuckin' queer! You're gonna get us busted!"

"I'm more worried your peanut head's gonna ruin the taste of the chocolate." Nathan picked it up from the ground, ripped the paper off and took a bite. "No, you're lucky; no lice penetrated the wrapper."

Debussy snickered, then finally declared loudly, "OK, let's have a picnic!" With heightened enthusiasm they made their way to their regular picnic sight, bringing a cart full of munchies. They stood next to the wooden, hollow bottomed fruit stands. Christopher shielded Nathan, as Nathan started throwing things under the stand. Debussy stood by acting like he was testing the watermelons for ripeness. Finally they emptied their cart.

Nathan peered around until no one was looking. He laid down and rolled underneath the ledge of the stand. Christopher moved the cart over to block the view. Nathan then climbed up into the center of the stand and crawled over the wooden wall, until he was down hidden away in the center. It camouflaged him completely. He could only see people's feet if they stood up against the stand. No one could see him though, unless they were to lay with their back on the floor and roll under the ledge. The center of the fruit stand made a ceiling about three and a half feet high, perfect for anyone sitting down to have a picnic.

After Nathan was inside, Debussy stayed watch while Christopher followed suit. Debussy waited quite a while until most of the shoppers went into the vegetable section. He stood there shaking the watermelon until the coast was clear. Luckily there were no workers in the fruit section; all stocking occurred late at night by part-time stock clerks.

He looked around quickly, dived down, rolled under the ledge, then climbed inside. Nathan was snorting through his nose trying to contain his laughter, after Debussy had whacked his head on the two-by-four divider that hung down from the stand's inner ceiling.

Christopher was doing his normal gesture-his finger to his lips, trying to quiet Nathan. Nathan responded by whacking Christopher's hand, in contempt of his cowardness. Christopher followed it by throwing a bag of chips at Nathan in protest.

Debussy rubbed his head, smiled and grabbed the bag of chips from Nathan. However, he preferred the healthier organic chips baked with sea salt, to these preservative-laced, commercial name brand ones, which Nathan and Christopher selected. He had read much about proper dieting and tried to eat foods that were as wholesome as possible. It was difficult to do though in this capitalist paradise, where everything was over packaged and super-processed.

His mother, Justine always shopped at the health food market on the other end of the shopping center. Nathan and Christopher didn't know the difference. They just ate whatever appealed to their taste buds. Usually they chose brands that their television commercial conditioning convinced them were the coolest-though often the least nutritious and always the most costly. Then again what did they care about cost? They weren't paying for these unwholesome products. They were just "consuming" them.

For drinks Debussy selected fresh squeezed orange juice, unpasteurized with all the live enzymes still intact. His friends preferred those name brand, carbonated, caffeine-laced sugar waters, which the commercial brain washers called "soft drinks." Debussy actually read the packages of the products he stole, making sure he didn't put anything unnatural in his body. He was probably the most conscientious shoplifter one would ever meet.

At times Nathan jokingly called him "Mr. Natural." Though Debussy never let ignorant comments bother him. He would respond proudly, "My body's a castle; I'll never pollute its grounds."

Debussy would combat Nathan's teasing by making fun of his selfish desire to pursue fame and fortune, two things Debussy knew never brought anyone happiness. He would say to Nathan, "I'd rather be a health nut than a wealth nut."

Nathan had dreams of being a big time drug dealer, or some other type of high paid businessman, driving a Lamborghini with beautiful women dangling on his arms. He always had some little scheme worked out to try to make money. But he was often too lazy to make much of it. He would take the plastic price tags off of the shelves, fold them in half, forming perfect squares that fit nicely into the quarter gumball machines. After a few tries he eventually would get one stuck. This would allow him to keep turning the knob, until all the gumballs were out of the machine. He would fill up an entire grocery bag and then sell them at school. Another scheme of his was to steal bottles of cinnamon oil from the pharmacy and toothpicks, dip them and sell the cinnamon picks at school.

***

In many ways Debussy was the complete antithesis of his friends. He longed for the day when he would meet someone who he could actually relate to, or rather could relate to him. Even when it came to drugs Debussy chose natural over synthetic. His friends occasionally experimented with synthetic drugs like LSD or Ecstasy. They also drank alcohol and smoked cigarettes. But from Debussy's studies he learned that marijuana was a far less dangerous and definitely healthier alternative to even alcohol or nicotine. And Debussy would definitely not partake in things he hadn't fully studied and learned were beneficial, or at least innocuous.

Debussy knew no one ever died from smoking a joint. Though he was disgustingly aware that some senseless people still believed the wild tales of that leader in yellow journalism, the notorious William Randolph Hearst invented some seventy or so years ago. He had read in *Hemp: Life Line to the Future* that Mr. Hearst was but one of the many moneyed interests who perpetuated the crazy myths about this so-called "Mexican Drug." Even years after they were exposed as lies, people still foolishly referred to Marijuana as a "dangerous narcotic." But this was of course a "smoke and mirrors" ploy to keep people ignorant of the real dangerous drugs like Nicotine, Caffeine, Cocaine and Alcohol.

Debussy read a book by the title, "*Smoke and Mirrors,*" which showed how Barry McCaffrey and others in the US state department's "War on Drugs" were fooling people about the real drug problems, namely those involving our government's complicity and the CIA's help. People who study the real issues of the America's drug problem are wise to refer to the CIA, as the "Cocaine Import Agency." Stupidly many people are locked in prisons for possessing very small amounts of marijuana, an otherwise harmless substance, while the real crooks are running this country and other client-states abroad.

Among Hearst's co-conspirators were the chemical madman, Dupont and the greedy oil tycoon, Rockefeller. We can all thank these three despicable thugs for the depletion of the ozone layer, the increase of green house gases and a host of other environmental disasters. In cahoots they all helped talk Henry Ford into not converting his model T into a clean burning hemp fueled automobile, but instead to keep it a polluting, gas guzzling, hell on wheels. They also helped ram the insane legislation through a lame-duck congress, which banned the most prosperous and beneficial industries in world history. Before this hemp was one the most widely used industrial materials worldwide.

Some of its seemingly infinite uses: The Constitution of the US, which along with all other paper documents of the time, was written on hemp paper. The Navy and all other marine vessels used hemp rope. Fiberboard made of hemp was widely used as a building product. Many types of glue were produced from hemp residues. During times of famine people throughout the world relied on hemp seeds, ground down into an oatmeal type substance for nourishment. It was one of the very few vegetable products that competed well for protein content with soy. Most of the clothing was made of hemp, including the first Levi's, which was not only longer lasting than the later cotton ones, but also far better for the environment. And the list goes on and on.

Thanks to Dupont and his chemicals (which were used to convert tree pulp into a cheaper, shorter lasting paper) and his poisonous bleaching agents, which continue to pollute the worlds last remaining clean water supplies, this new, impure "white paper" was pushed onto an unknowing society, who believed all their capitalist propaganda. Of course they weren't the only ones who bought into the insanity. Textile companies knew they could dominate new markets with their flimsier manufactured garments. The "built in obsolescence" was an added benefit to those who could sell and resell you things, which in the past lasted nearly forever.

The greed and ignorance inherent in capitalism showed no end. A destructive plant that depleted the soil and left land nearly unfarmable soon replaced a plant that grew naturally, often in the wild, which anchored and nourished the soil. The famous dust bowls of the south were just one example of the folly of this historical tragedy. A plant that consumed more carbon dioxide than it released while burning, was replaced by fuel that drastically increased the levels of carbon dioxide in the air. This helped contribute to increased green house gases and to the drastic climate changes that followed.

Debussy saw how, even in its inchoate stages capitalism had major deleterious effects on the natural world. And if this behavior wasn't stopped, it could make the planet uninhabitable in the future.

***

Debussy in no way wanted to support this move from the natural to the artificial and destructive, not even while he was stoned with the munchies.

White Lies

Debussy's desire to smoke out started decreasing as his hunger for knowledge and meaning grew. He took more books from his father's collection-writings from and about Socrates, Gandhi, Martin Luther King Jr., Steven Biko, Malcolm X, Che Guevara, Jose Marti and other revolutionary figures. He started to realize by studying historical movements that although education seemed to be the slowest means to social change, it also appeared to be the only lasting means. Debussy saw how corrupt officials and large corporations that benefited from the status quo tried their hardest to keep people ignorant and powerless. Big corporate ownership of the mainstream media was one of the surest ways the establishment kept people misinformed.

It wasn't what people didn't know that was the problem. It's what they know that isn't so. He knew that if other people were aware of the brutal realities of the current world, they too would become outraged and demand change. He wanted to somehow, someway share with others what he had discovered from his dad's book collection. If his dad were still alive he was sure he would want the same.

At the end of the first week of school the students were given card stock paper to cover their textbooks as a weekend homework assignment. Debussy spent Sunday evening covering his books and drawing pictures on the covers. In a large black marker he changed the names of the subjects to words better described his impression of their contents, after briefly scanning them. On his history book he wrote in bold, "White Lies!" On his geography book he wrote, "Euro-American-Centricity!" On the Math book he wrote, "Robotic Brain-Washing!"

He also drew great pictures that augmented his new chosen titles. On the "White Lies" book he drew a picture of Martin Luther King Jr. being assassinated in front of a brick wall that was adorned with spray paint, which exclaimed, "Ask Not What Your Country Has Done to The World!" On the cover of the book, which he titled "Euro-American-Centricity" he drew a map of the United States in the top left-hand corner and a map of Europe in the top right-hand corner. From each continent he drew dangling handcuffs with strangle holds on maps of both Latin America and Africa respectively. On the book he titled "Robot Brain-Washing," he drew a large calculator with robots with outstretched hands hopping from button to button. The Robots had captions coming from their mouths, which read, "Same Place. Same

Thing." In later years, he would call Civics, "American Political Indoctrination" and Science, "Western Materialism." For Economics he would use the title, "Neo-liberal, Capitalist Propaganda."

On the next day of school Debussy carried his books proudly, hoping someone would question them, so he would be able to strike up a conversation about the issues he was attempting to address. He walked through the locker bay. As he approached his locker, Lori Thompson was getting her books out of the locker two above his. She shared her locker with a few other girl friends, so the locker was crammed with books. As she was busy sorting through them, he slowly approached from behind. He wanted desperately to get her attention. He couldn't think of anything to say. So he said, "ah, excuse me." She didn't even look or respond verbally. She simply moved her legs a little to the side so he could get to his locker. As he bent down he could smell her perfume. His shoulder was inches from her tanned, freshly shaven legs. She wore a short flowered, summer dress, which clung beautifully to her firm body. Her light brown hair was up in a French braid.

As Debussy turned the combination, his heart beat fast and his breath grew heavy. He thought of what he could say. "How are you doing?" Or maybe something shorter-"Hello" perhaps. While he was contemplating his delivery she pulled a book out, causing two atop it to come tumbling down. One landed on his shoulder. And the other hit the back of his head. She said, "oh, sorry!" as he handed her the fallen books.

The only remark that came to his mind was, "It's all right, ah, I have two shoulders." Here was his opportunity to start talking to her. But he couldn't even look her in the eyes. When he handed the books to her he became speechless. She snatched them from him, grabbed the books she needed, hurriedly shut her locker and walked off saying, "sorry" once more.

He just kneeled down and watched her leave in regret. He couldn't even try to say "bye" or let her know he knew her name. He believed, to her he was just another boy in the locker room. Even though she too was a freshman, she seldom associated with freshman guys. He blew another perfect chance. In disappointment he got up, took his "White Lies" book and proceeded to history class.

***

"Gregory?"

"Here."

"Jackson?"

"Here."

"Jensen?"

"Yeah?" he said nonchalantly.

"That's 'here' Jensen!" Mr. Cranston demanded fascistically.

"OK, but actually the name's Debut." He grunted back.

"No Mr. Jensen. You say the word 'here!' or you'll be marked absent." Now getting even louder.

"Here, sir!" Debussy belted out, using his best military impression, accompanied by a Nazi hand salute, mocking Mr. Cranston's authoritarianism. Luckily, Mr. Cranston was looking down at his roll book, didn't notice Debussy's solute and moved on.

"Kerres?"

"Here."

"Lehnert?"

"Here."

"Matthews?"

"Ah, here."

"Miller?"

"Here."

"Phelps?"

"Here, sir!" Equally as loud as Debussy's salute. Nathan winked over at Debussy with a half smile. Debussy smiled back. They were sitting two seats apart from each other in the back of the room, both with perfect views of Lori Thompson, who sat a few seats closer to the middle of the class. She was still finishing last night's homework assignment-writing the name on the cover of her book.

"Richter?"

"Ah, here."

"Shimamoto?"

"Here."

"Tanners?"

"Here."

"Thompson?" Debussy looked over at her to see how she would respond.

She put down her marker, looked up slowly and said, in a seductive voice, "here, sir." She wasn't purposely copying Debussy or Nathan's comments. She always used cordial greetings such as "sir" and "ma'am." She was the daughter of the city mayor, Anthony

Thompson. She displayed the most formal manners, especially in formal institutions where others viewing her might have contact with her father.

"Vaughn?"

"Here."

As Lori picked up her marker to resume her assignment, she bent down slightly and out of the corner of her eye she noticed Debussy staring. He quickly looked away and cleared his throat nervously. She too got a little embarrassed and looked away. She realized for the first time that this was the guy who had the locker under hers. She still was embarrassed for dropping books on him.

"Dude, she was checking you out." Laughed Nathan over his shoulder, in a whisper.

"Shut up." Debussy got a little red, realizing Nathan was watching him drool over Lori.

"OK class. Let's get started. So I see you got your book all covered nicely Miss Thompson?" Mr. Cranston paced up and down the isles eye-balling everyone's textbook, to make sure they did their weekend assignments. Lori folded her hands neatly over the cover of her book to hide the fact she hadn't finished titling it. "So Mr. Phelps, where's your book?"

Nathan responded matter-of-factly. "It's below my chair, underneath my folder."

"Well, you care if I see the cover?"

"Ah, I don't see why not." He fumbled with his notebook, not retrieving any hoped for book. "Ah, actually, I must have accidentally left it in my friend's mom's car, on the way to school this morning." He never got a ride to school, but it was a great try.

Mr. Cranston scrunched up his nose and forehead, squinted through his eyeglasses at his grade book and chortled, "Well I guess one incomplete won't kill you." As he waved his pencil in the air like Zorro, the Gay Blade, all proud of his power over his students, he swooshed it down over the grade book, drawing a nice big check mark next to Nathan's name. "Ah." He took off his glasses and proceeded to circle to the back of the room.

Debussy folded his hands over his book like Lori, covering the title he wrote. Although he wanted his classmates to see that he wrote, "White Lies" on the book, he didn't care to challenge his teacher's stubbornness in front of his classmates. He already saw how difficult it was just trying to get Mr. Cranston to use his first name. He passed

Debussy. Debussy gave a fake smile. Then Mr. Cranston proceeded to the front of the room, as Debussy let out a relieved sigh.

"OK. Where did we leave off last week? Miss Anderson?"

"We were talking about Columbus sailing the ocean blue in fourteen ninety two." She recited like a famous song-all proud of herself.

Debussy whispered over to Nathan in disgust, "In fourteen ninety-three Columbus stole all he could see."

"Mr. Jensen! Do you have something to share with the entire class?"

"Ah, no Mr. Cranston. I was just asking Nathan if he wanted to look off my book, since he forgot his." It was a great recovery.

"Oh, isn't that nice of you." Mocking Debussy in a whining voice. "Why don't we have Nathan come up to the front of the room and sit next to Miss Anderson? I'm sure he could use a little tutoring. And Mr. Jensen, I'll have you fill in the empty chair next to Miss Thompson, so I can keep a better eye on the both of you."

They both got up. As they crossed each other's path Nathan whispered, "What a prick."

Debussy's face was flushed with embarrassment. He wanted to be next to Lori. But this was a little too close for comfort. After just clobbering him in the head with her textbooks, she too felt the discomfort.

Both Nathan and Trisha Anderson had aversions to each other. Although she wasn't bad looking with her glasses on, she was way too stiff for Nathan's liking.

"So let's back up and talk about Prince Henry the Navigator of Portugal. Henry discovered Madeira and the Azores and sent out ships to circumnavigate Africa for the first time."

Debussy sat back and listened in amazement, thinking: "God where did this quack get his education?" Debussy knew that the Afro-Phoenicians sailed all the way around Africa before 600 BCE. But instead his textbook credited Bartholomew Dias with being the first to round the Cape of Good Hope, at the southern tip of Africa in 1488-completely omitting the accomplishments of the Afro-Phoenicians.

He knew from reading the book *Lies My Teacher Told Me; Everything Your American History Text Books Got Wrong*, by James Loewen that the ancient Phoenicians and Egyptians voyaged as far as Ireland and England, reaching Madeira and Azores and conducted trade with aborigines in the Canary Islands. "What, just because the white man was able to duplicate the accomplishment two thousand years later, that makes the original navigators' accomplishments obsolete? Just because they weren't white?" He thought to himself in anger.

As Loewen put it in his eye-opening book, "omitting the accomplishments of the Afro-Phoenicians is ironic, because it was Prince Henry's knowledge of their feats that inspired him to replicate them." It seemed so absurd that Debussy's corporate textbook manufacturers viewed all modern technology as a European development. The Afro-Phoenicians' accomplishments did not conform to the invented story line his school system wanted to brainwash the kids with, about how "white" Europeans taught the rest of the world how to do things.

Disillusionment

The weekend before when Debussy was scanning his textbook, he couldn't believe there was no mention of the Muslims preserving Greek wisdom of sailing and enhancing it with knowledge from China, India and Africa, or how they passed it on to Europe via Spain. Instead his book showed Henry inventing navigation, and that "before Europe there was nothing"-at least nothing "modern."

When the bell rang he was glad his hypnosis session was finally over. And fortunately his sanity was still intact. As everyone began exiting, Debussy just sat there with his head down thinking, "Man can I take four more years of this crap?"

Nathan woke him with a flick on the ear. "Come on, you got to get to your Geometry class."

"When did you start fuckin' caring about getting to class on time?" Debussy barked back with abhorrence. Everyone was willing to just go on with their day, completely oblivious to the lies being fed them. "Am I the only person in this damn school who has some sense of reality?" He thought. He knew it was helpless to discuss the matter with Nathan, who didn't know his head from his ass.

"You just let your girl walk out without you." Joked Nathan.

"I got to go to a doctor's appointment." Debussy replied, not even hearing or caring what Nathan just said.

"What are you sick?"

"Huh? Ah, no. Just a check up." Answered Debussy, completely disinterested as he walked out into the square-into the blinding sunlight, which seemed to pierce through the fury he felt. Luckily the sun was one sign of truth in this fake town. The cloud of lies that surrounded this school would never fool the sun.

"What, you think you got AIDS or something?" Nathan laughed, as they parted-Debussy completely tuning him out.

This was the start of his regular excuses. He would later have doctor's appointments, dentist appointments, family emergencies. He thought up all kinds of reasons to ditch classes. Debussy became proficient at forging letters from his mother, to justify his absences from school.

He started visiting the city library at least two to three times per week-hiding away in the sounds of the flowing waterfall. It soothed his jaded thoughts. He continued sneaking into the garage to visit his father's book collection, seeking solace from a backward and hypocritical society. Unfortunately, these books only left him further perplexed and upset with his world.

Soon he became completely disillusioned by his studies of social, political and historical issues. Was there nothing he could believe in? He began wondering, "Perhaps it would be easier to just stay ignorant and try to forget all I know." He tried this. He laid back on the grass by the lake in Central Park and tried desperately to clear his mind and just enjoy the sound of the birds. But soon the police helicopter bussed by like a vulture. It broke his trance.. After repeated attempts failed to keep the many voices of the millions who were daily being used by his country's colonial and capitalistic ways from prying their way back into his memory, he soon abandoned trying to remain apathetic. He just couldn't do it. It wasn't in his nature. How the masses pulled it off, he couldn't fathom.

Eventually he started yearning for something deeper-something spiritual perhaps. He felt there must be some deeper meaning to life, which made life worth living-something that made sense of all the insanity he was confronted with. He remembered reading Duncan Sheik's lyrics. "Every holocaust has meaning. Not set in stone, but drawn in sand." What did this mean?

His dad had a great mélange of books in his collection on religion and spirituality. He wondered what his dad believed. How did he keep his sanity with all he knew? He gathered some of the book he'd previously tossed aside. He took a whole bag: The *Lost Years of Jesus, Dreaming the Dark, The Seat of the Soul, The Celestine Prophesies, The Tibetan Book of the Dead, Many Lives Many Masters*, *Unlocking the Mysteries of Birth and Death* and a few others. He started reading through them. His hunger for wisdom caused him to skip around from book to book. He thought Starhawk's book about the "Religion of the Goddess" was interesting and empowering. Yet somehow he felt it left too many questions unresolved. Brian Weiss's book about past life regressions made him feel a sense of peace, knowing death was just another doorway. But when he came to Ho Goku's book, *Unlocking the Mysteries of Birth and Death*, he couldn't put it down. It was the only book he read from cover to cover. In fact, he was even considering reading it a second time-a thing he never did. On his first reading, he took it down to Central Park, sat under a tree by the lake and became completely engulfed in it.

He always believed Buddhism was about bald headed, orange robed men who sat cross-legged and meditated. "How could that change his life or the world?" He thought. This Buddhism was worlds different from the misconception he previously held. Ho Goku described this as a living Buddhism, a philosophy that empowered people to change their lives and in turn transform the world around them from the inside out. Unlike his studies of Western religions, which spoke of something outside of life, which possessed absolute power and wisdom-some god or force-from what Debussy started to understand, it seemed that this Buddhism taught that life itself was omnipotent and omniscient. He was also led to believe that it was possible to harness this power and wisdom (which is naturally inherent in his life) and use it to direct his life in a positive, meaningful direction. Ho Goku's book also taught him that he could influence others to do the same. Ho Goku called this process a "Human Revolution." As he put it, "the human revolution of a single individual could change the destiny of the entire world."

It all sounded nice. But he had his doubts. Why did he never hear this take on Buddhism before? Why did his culture seem to portray Buddhism as a dead religion, which belonged in caves and monasteries? He went to Wutherington Beach Library to see if they had other books by Ho Goku. He found two children's books in Japanese. That wouldn't help him.

So the next day he decided to visit one of those humongous bookstore chains, one fully loaded with the coffeehouse upstairs. He ascended the escalator to the second floor where he found three whole shelves on Eastern thought. He searched through a plethora of Zen books, books on Tibetan Buddhism, the Dalia Lama's books on meditation and the like. As he scanned through them, none seemed to give him the same satisfaction Ho Goku's book did. But nowhere could he find a book by Ho Goku, or even books on the subjects Ho Goku wrote about-The Lotus Sutra or the Buddhism of Nichiren.

"Damn how could this guy just write one book this good and not write more?" He thought. He walked up to a cute, young lady who was sorting and putting away books. Noticing her nametag, he said politely, "ah, excuse me, Jessica, can you help me find a certain author I'm having trouble locating?"

She smiled hesitantly, looked down at her nametag and looked back up. "Sure, what's the author's name?" She seemed amused that this stranger called her by name.

"Goku, ah, Ho Goku."

"Ho Goku?" I've never heard of him. "What has he written?"

"Well I read one of his books-*Unlocking the Mystery of Birth and Death.* And I found two children's books in Japanese at the library."

"What does he write about?"

"The Buddhism of Nichiren. It's based on the Lotus Sutra."

"Sounds interesting. Are you doing a report for school?"

"No I just liked the book and I want to read more like it."

"Well we have a section over here on Eastern thought." She started walking to the area he just left. Although he already thoroughly searched those shelves, he followed the scent of her perfume without protesting. He enjoyed watching her perform the same routine he had completed just moments ago, knowing she wouldn't find anything he hadn't found. She was a sight to see kneeling down in her brown corduroy skirt and black tights. She kept grabbing her long, dark, wavy hair and pulling it over one shoulder, to keep it from falling in her face. "Ah, I guess I can't find anything by that author. We do have many other Buddhist authors here."

"I know, too many. I already scanned through them and I didn't see any I cared for-none that were as good as Ho Goku's."

"Let me check our computer." She walked over to the computerized card catalog and typed in "Goku."

"Author not found. Huh. OK, let me check in the publisher's computer for any works he has published." She once again typed in "Goku." A long list popped up. Many of the books had "Unavailable" or "Out of Print" listed after the title in the status column. Many of the titles indicated they were printed in a few different languages, most of them in Japanese and English, some also in Spanish, Italian, German and French. There were even a couple printed in Vietnamese, Chinese and Korean. She pushed enter and another page came up with more books by him. There were many dialogues with prominent people such as, Linus Pauling, Arnold Toynbee, Chandra Wickramasinghe, Johan Galtung and others.

The titles seemed endless: *A Lasting Peace, A Lifelong Quest for Peace, Before it's Too Late, Buddhism and the Cosmos, Buddhism the First Millennium, Choose Peace, Dawn After Dark, Dialogue on Life, Dialogue on Youth, Life; An Enigma a Precious Jewel*, *Man Himself Must Choose, Songs From My Heart*, *Space and Eternal Life, The Flower of Chinese Buddhism, Today Tomorrow and Yesterday, Unlocking the Mystery of Birth and Death* and on and on....

After she pushed enter and a third page of his books came up, they both looked at each other bewildered and amazed. "Well I guess he hasn't written enough books to qualify for this corporate mega-store." Debussy said jokingly.

She didn't know how to explain. There seemed to be more books written by this author than Hemingway, Steinbeck and Twain combined. "I don't know what to say; I guess I can order some for you, if you'd like."

"No it's OK. I'll check some other stores." They both smiled, and Debussy left saying, "Good bye."

She answered with a wave, "Bye." They both looked back at each other as he was leaving.

Winter

Soon fall gave way to winter's ominous grip. As the California rain washed away the polluted sky, Debussy yearned to be cleansed of all the confusion he felt. However, cleansing wisdom seemed hard to attain on his own. How the day's dragged on. No libraries, no bookstores in all of Orange County carried any Ho Goku books. Was his searching in vain?

He kept looking at the name penciled in the back of his father's book: "Theodore Copeland," and the number accompanying it: "872-4871." He felt sure the number no longer existed. However he kept wondering if this guy-if he was locatable-knew anything about the author of this book, or about his father.

Finally his curiosity drove him to action. He called the number. Sure enough he got a disconnected signal. He then called information, but there was no listing for the name in either Orange, Los Angeles, San Bernardino, or San Diego counties. Just as he was about to give up on the entire idea, he thought of checking the internet at the library.

The following day after school he took the bus to his favorite hang out, The Wutherington Beach Library. He signed on one of the computers to search e-mail addresses. After many different searches he found it: tcopeland@scv.org. He got very excited. "Maybe this guy can tell me how my dad died?" he thought. A feeling of submissive nihilism followed the thought. "This guy's not going to remember my dad." Feeling he had nothing left to loose he signed up for a free email address and sent Theodore an e-mail letter.

Hi Theodore,

I don't know how or if you knew my dad, Christopher Xanthankis. But I found your name and an old phone number written in the back of one of his books by Ho Goku, entitled *Unlocking the Mystery of Birth and Death.* I found the book very interesting. And I hoped you might know how I can find out more about his writings.

Thank You, Debut X

A week later he finally received a reply.

Debut,

Sorry it took a while. I rarely check my work e-mail. I remember when you were born. Your father and I were working on an educational radio program, which we were bringing to other countries. Your father had to leave in the middle of one of the tapings to go to the hospital, where your mother was in labor with you.

How old are you now? I only knew your dad a short while. I introduced him to the Buddhism of Nichiren. He practiced it on and off for a short while, but wasn't really that consistent. He was also trying many other religious practices at the time.

How's your brother and mom doing? I'm glad to hear you liked Ho Goku's book. He's one of my favorite authors. I have many more of his books. They are hard to come by in bookstores. But I can loan you any of them. You can also come to a Buddhist introduction meeting if you'd like.

Give me a call at 714-894-7288.

Take care, T.C.

He hurried home extremely excited. He couldn't wait to call Theodore. Someone actually knew his dad. He never spoke to anyone else who knew Charles, except his mother. But she never said anything. As if he'd never existed, his name wasn't mentioned in the house. His father's side of the family lived on the East Coast. Debussy's mother never had the money to travel there. And it appeared his father's family was in the same boat.

The bus seemed to be going slower than usual. Or was it just he was more conscious of the time now? Many people were coming home from work; the bus kept stopping. He stared out the window watching the trees pass, thinking of what he would ask Theodore. "How did my father die?" Perhaps. Maybe not those exact words-too direct. "What did my father believe in?"

The bus putted on, picking up day laborers coming home from a hard day's work. The smell of sweat surrounded him. He recognized a few of the workers who lived in his apartments. There was soon only standing room. He thought to himself, "Shit, hurry up already!"

The landscape changed from town homes, to parks, to apartments. Soon they drove by the Wutherington Beach Police Station. He always felt angry passing this building. It gave him a lump in his throat, which he couldn't suppress. His thoughts drifted back to last summer and the riots the police instigated. He had been thinking a lot about last Fourth of July.

***

When he closed his eyes he was once again running down that dark alley, surrounded by a throng of teenagers. They were fleeing baton wielding police officers who were trying to force crowds of teenagers out of the downtown area. As they approached the end of the alley another swarm of kids came from the other direction, running perpendicular to his group, on a collision course with each other.

Crisscrossing each other they tried not to collide-though a few did. A girl just a few paces ahead of Debussy tripped and skinned her knees. He heard her call out as she fell. Debussy put his hand out to help her up, while trying to not get trampled by the stampede of teenagers.

She blocked her face as a few jumped over her. One accidentally kneed Debussy's shoulder. As he regained his footing, he felt a stinging mist shower over him. His eyes began to burn. He stumbled to the side of the alley, laid down behind some trashcans and tried to wipe his eyes, to clear his vision. He heard what sounded like a line of galloping horses, then just the sound of yelling kids slowly receding into the distance. Soon all he could hear was the sounds of sirens blocks away.

***

The bus came to an abrupt stop, startling Debussy from his daydream. He looked out the window and noticed he was a few stops past his apartments. He rang the bell and exited the bus, walking a few streets back to his apartment.

He climbed the steps, took out his key and opened the door. His mom was at work as usual. Zeus was out at a friend's probably. This was the perfect opportunity to call Theodore, without anyone knowing or butting in.

He quickly punched in the numbers: 8 9 4 7 2 8 8. His heart started to beat loudly. He still hadn't decided what he would say. After a few rings the call transferred to a voice mail. "Hello. Ya've reached 894-7288. Sorry, I can come ta da phone right now. Please leave a message, an aw call ya right back as soon as possible."

He left a brief message, "Ah, this is Debut. Ah, give me a call at 714-960-2806. Ah, thanks." He hung up in disappointment and shrunk back on the couch, starring at the wall. He was thinking about everything. Then again he was thinking about nothing. Soon his eyes started to follow a cockroach, as it crawled along the tiled wall in the adjoining kitchen. He didn't even think to kill them anymore. It's as if they'd just become part of his home, like the holes in the walls formed by the door handles smacking them repeatedly.

Although he hated these rundown apartments and wished he could move somewhere nicer, he no longer hated the cockroaches. He was sure they hated it there just as much. If he were to open a cereal box and one or two fell out, he would simply brush them aside and go on with his own business.

He pulled out one of the library books from his bag and started to read. It was that book by Gary Webb about the connection between the CIA, the Contras and the crack cocaine explosion in LA in the 80's. He was reading the story about "Freeway" Ricky Ross and how he got his start in the crack business, when suddenly the phone rang out, splitting through the silence like an ax though a log of wood.

"Ah, hello?" He said startled.

"Hi is dis Debussy?"

"Yeah." With less hesitation.

"Sorry, I's in my office doin' some work and didn't hear ma private line."

"T.C.?"

"Yeah. How ya doing?"

"Ah, good."

"You're probably too young ta remember me. You's just a little tike when I saw ya lass. So how's da famly doin'?"

"Oh they're good. They're out right now."

"So ya'v been readin' some'a yo fatha's books huh?"

"Yeah. But my mom doesn't know. I snuck'em out of the garage. They've been packed away since he died." He paused, hoping Theodore would volunteer a comment about his father's death. They were both silent for what seemed an eternity to Debussy. He was struck numb and couldn't talk.

Then finally Theodore slowly broke the silence. "So ya interested in readin' some mow a Ho Goku's books huh?"

"Yeah!"

"Well, I can eitha drop'em off at yo place. Or you can come by my place some time and pick'em up."

"I'd rather come by your place. I don't want my mom to wonder what I'm getting into. Parents always manage to think the worst of things."

"Aint dat da troof. Alright, well when da ya wanna come ova?"

Debussy didn't want to seem anxious, although he was, very. "Well when are you available?"

"Les see, I work out a my house in da day time, writin' an studyin'. In da evenin's I usually go ta Buddhist gatherin's, or workout at da gym. I host a public radio show on Thursday nights, so I usually spen' most'a da afternoon dare, preparin' fo da show. On Mondays, I do some assistant editin' work fo a monthly Buddhist magazine. But any other afternoon, after ya get out a school, you can stop by. I'm usually here. Jus call befo' ya come by."

"OK great. I'll give you a call."

He hung up the phone but wished he hadn't. He wanted to talk more. Possibly set up a time this week to see him. He didn't want to appear too anxious though. He picked up the phone again, started to dial.

"No." He hung it up again.

Spring

Two months later, Debussy finally got the courage up to call Theodore back and set a time to visit him. "Hi. T.C.?"

"Well Well. I'd been waitin' fo you ta call. So when ya gonna come visit me?" Theodore knew that it took a lot for a person to get connected to this Buddhism. In one parable from the sutras, Shakyamuni relates that it's as rare to run into the Lotus Sutra as it would be for a one eyed turtle to find a piece of sandal wood floating on the surface of the water the right size for him to rest on.

During the whole two months that Debussy waited to call Theodore back, he had spent his days alone-not reading as he usually did, not smoking pot with his friends, or shop lifting-instead just thinking about life and all he had read since his discovery. He spent the days laying by the lake at central park, staring at the clouds, watching them drift by-imagining his life drifting by with those clouds. What is life? Is it anything anyone could ever fully comprehend? He had read in Ho Goku's book that the universe was infinite, that the entire universe was pregnant with the possibility for life.

Shakyamuni spoke about many Buddha lands throughout the universe. At night he would lay down in the field across from his house and stare at the few visible stars. He'd wonder if there were other civilizations that had learned how to end war and end exploitation by one race over others, or one class of men over another and learned to live in harmony. Buddhism says that all of life's problems arise from the "Three Poisons:" Greed, Anger and Ignorance. Had some civilization out there learned how to suppress those poisons and direct them toward the betterment of all?

Sometimes people's lives aren't ready for the drastic change that would accompany meeting the Lotus Sutra. Inevitably they always run into obstacles that prevent them from discovering things that are really good for them. Their karma draws them again and again to that which makes them miserable. Theodore just waited patiently, chanted and had faith Debussy would call him when the time was right. It was actually Debussy's searching that brought Theodore into his life.

"Well, ah, I'm free tomorrow afternoon."

"Great. I had a meetin' dat just canceled. How bout I come pick ya up from school?"

"Can you drop me back off at the library afterwards? I can take the bus home from there."

"Sure. If dat's bess fo you? Ya go da Wutherington Beach High, right?"

"Yeah. I can meet you at the bus stop in front of school on Main Street, if that's OK?"

"Perfect. What time?"

"I ah, get out of school at 2:30. How about 2:45?"

"OK. Awl be dare."

"Alright. I'll see you tomorrow. Thanks."

"OK take care Debut."

"Bye."

Debussy hung up the phone and took a deep breath. He felt nervous. Then again he was excited. Why did he feel so hopeful, yet so apprehensive at the same time about meeting this stranger? They say, "When the student is ready, the teacher will appear." Would this man, whom Debussy presumed by his accent was an older African American man, be the teacher he was looking for, to help him understand this perplexing world and all of its endless contradiction?

He feverishly rushed through the day hoping he could cause it to pass quicker. The weather seemed mysterious. Although it was almost spring now, clouds covered the sky, as if it would rain, though rain never fell. A misty breeze blew leaves from the trees, reminding Debussy of last fall, when he thought he would never be able to bare another day in the compound of Wutherington Beach High. Spring was just beginning to creep up upon them. He could taste the salt water in the air from blocks away. He knew he would soon be swimming in the lovely waters of the Pacific. Being a Pisces he lived for this time of year.

Mentor

As Debussy entered Theodore's house, he was led through a few different rooms. Each was representative of a different culture. He first went through a Japanese room with tatami mats and a Buddhist altar, with pictures of ancient Japanese castles and dignified looking Japanese men and women, whom Debussy didn't recognize. Then he went through a Native American room with a buffalo fur on the floor, all different Native American artifacts on tables, and Native American art and pictures of Native Americans, of whom Debussy only recognized Sitting Bull. Finally they went into his study, which was decorated in an African motif. He had bookshelves circling the room and pictures on the walls of famous revolutionary African and African American figures, such as Nelson Mandela, Steven Biko, Malcolm X, Martin Luther King, Jr. and Rosa Parks.

He asked Debussy to take a seat in one of the many couch chairs, which also circled the room and make himself at home. "So ya've enjo'ed *Unlockin' da Mysteries of Birf and Deaf*, huh?" Theodore wore a warm smile and seemed to look deeply into Debussy. "One a my favorite books by 'im is *Life; An Enigma, A Precious Jewel*."

Theodore's beautiful house and all its incredible decorations amazed Debussy. He felt very comfortable with Theodore. He was a towering, well build African American man, who looked to be in his late forties. One could tell by one glance that he definitely worked out regularly. Debussy took a breath and commented, "It's strange, but the way Ho Goku explains Buddhism in this book reminded me of what I've always kind of believed about life. But I just couldn't explain it so eloquently, or systematize my beliefs in such a perfect fashion. In my mind I've always simply jumbled up a bunch of parts of different beliefs. I take only those that make sense and haven't been disproved by science, or don't contradict common sense and logic-which much of what I've studied about western religion seems to."

Theodore leaned back in his chair folding his arms, doing his best imitation of Yoda meditating and spoke slowly in reply to Debussy. "Since alw religious beliefs 'originally' originated from da minds a' people, trying dare bess to esplain ultimate reality- and human consciousness in an enlighten' state has da potential a' perceiving ultimate troofs-many religions contain partial aspects of de ultimate troof. Now I say 'originally' 'cause religions have gone from peopo tryin' to esplain reality, to leada's tryin' ta justify dare control ova peopo'. But as peopo' become mo enlighten', day'll perceive mo a da ultimate troof, or as day say, 'reality in itself.' Shakyamuni, or prince Siddhartha, da historical Buddha of India from about 500+ BCE was simply de firs', on dis planet at leas', or dat we ha' record of anyways, who became fully enlighten' to dis ultimate reality.

"Shakyamuni understood dat awl peopo possessed de ability ta become enlighten'-dat awl peopo' are in fac Buddhas in de process a discoverin' dare 'Buddha Nature,' or dare inherent enlightenment. In da final years a his life, he eventually felt enough of his successors were finally ready ta excep' dis troof, so he taught his final teachin's, da Lotus Sutra.

"Here Debut, read what Shakyamuni says ta his greates' successors in da Lotus Sutra."

Debussy picked up the Lotus Sutra and read out the part Theodore was pointing to, "Shariputra, you should know that at the start I took a vow, hoping to make all persons equal to me, without any distinction between us..."

"Ya see Debut, da Lotus Sutra represents da highes' form a democracy. Unfortunately, he knew dat da average person of his time wouldn't be ready fo' dis revolutionary idea fo' some millennia to come. So fo dis purpose he predicts dat 'Bodhisattva Superior Practice' will emerge in da 'Latter Day a da Law' an' lead da millions a' Bodhisattvas a' de Earf to awake wit-in dare fella Earflin's da 'Wondrous Law a da Lotus Blossom,' which is dare latent Buddha Nature, or dare highes' potential.

"Debut, we's in da 'Latter day a da Law' right now, an 'Bodhisattva Superior Practice' was Nichiren, who brought us da 'Wondrous Law a da Lotus Blossom' or Myo-ho Ren-ge Kyo. Shakyamuni says dis 'Wondrous Law a da Lotus Blossom' will spreads fo some ten thousan years an mo, on inta da future."

Debussy was normally the most skeptical person. He rarely believed what anyone said, unless it was backed by undeniable proof. Despite that, somehow he felt Theodore was speaking straight from his life, from actually years of experience. He could sense Theodore's unflinching integrity. He was moved by his life-force, which emanated with compassion. He also felt that coming from an African American, who obviously was in tune with the thoughts of some of Debussy's favorite revolutionaries that his belief in Buddhism had so much more credibility, than any other person talking about the greatness of their religion. After all, this would appear to be a religion that was foreign to Theodore's background. What was it about this Buddhism that made Theodore speak of it with such conviction? Debussy had to know.

Debussy wanted to find out as much as he could from Theodore. So he continued to probe into his mind with question after question. "I've read a lot about the corruption in our government and in big business, and of the destruction capitalism is causing around the world. I've usually been turned off to religion, because I've never believed it could do anything to change the glut of corruption and exploitation in the world. What can one practicing Buddhism do to change this prevailing system of corruption in American and the world at large?"

"Le me ha' ya read some a wa' Ho Goku says about Nichiren and Shakyamuni Buddha dis monf in au *Livin' Buddhism* Magazine."

Debussy read aloud the section Theodore had highlighted in the *Living Buddhism* magazine, in an article entitled "Dialogue on the Lotus Sutra."

> I think we could say that Nichiren Daishonin and Shakyamuni were revolutionaries of the most radical and fundamental kind. Shakyamuni toppled the prevalent notion that 'people exist for the sake of the gods,' teaching instead that 'the gods exist for the sake of the people.' At the same time, he rejected the Brahman caste, which arrogantly took advantage of people's belief, and the caste system itself. Proclaiming that all people are equal, he proceeded to put that assertion into practice....
>
> But in later times, the adherents of Buddhism forgot Shakyamuni's spirit, and consequently Buddhism ceased to be a humanistic teaching.
>
> It was then that Nichiren Daishonin appeared, declaring that people don't exist for the sake of the Buddha; rather, the Buddha exists for the sake of the people....
>
> Since religion is the very foundation of society it is a revolution in the realm of religion that will rectify all of society's ills on a fundamental level.

"Now he goes on ta relate dis attitude ta modern society an' says wha's needed is a 'human revolution.' We gotta change da way we value da common peopo'. In Buddhism, da common peopo' are supreme. Buddhism is de ultimate humanism, and da highest reasonin' about life. Now read wha' he says here about da backwardness of modern society's notions about how ta respect otha' peopo'."

Debussy continued to read aloud:

> I heard someone make the following argument: "Fundamentally, doctors exist to serve patients. It is their effort on behalf of patients that makes them doctors. Yet, all too often, doctors arrogantly think themselves superior to their patients.
>
> "Lawyers exist to help those facing legal troubles. Yet often lawyers become haughty, thinking themselves better than others.
>
> "Politicians exist for the sake of citizens. They are public servants. Yet politicians tend to grow insolent, supposing themselves above their constituents, whom they exploit.
>
> "The role of journalists should be to protect the rights of the people. Yet the mass media is sometimes at the forefront in violating those rights.
>
> "Clergy exist for the sake of the faithful. Yet it happens that priests think of themselves as higher, asserting superiority over believers."

"You see Debut, da mission of da 'Bodhisattvas of da earf' is ta turn ova dees foolish notions of some peopo' bein' above otha' peopo'. And reassert da dignity a' awl life. Because peopo' begrudge dare life an' other's lives, dats why we's in da predicament we's in. Also peopo don't respect Motha Earf, day foolishly believe dat Motha Earf belongs to dem, instead of realizin' dat day belong ta Motha Earf."

***

After talking with Theodore for a couple of hours, Debussy received enough to chew on for a year or two. He went away totally empowered, with new hope for humanity, with a new aspiration to study and exert himself as a "Bodhisattva of the Earth," to awaken this "Wondrous Law of the Lotus Blossom" within his own life, which Theodore helped enlighten him to. Without questioning, he immediately went home and alone in his room began invoking aloud the "Wondrous Law of the Lotus Blossom"-reciting the very title of this great sutra. "Nam Myo-ho Ren-ge Kyo. Nam Myo-ho Ren-ge Kyo. Nam Myo-ho Ren-ge Kyo." As he kept saying it, slowly tears of joy flowed from his heart. He had never felt such elation coming from his life. Finally their was something which gave his life meaning, that gave him hope he could, along with others eventually transform this muddy swamp of chaos and dissolution into a flower garden of Lotus Blossoms.

Human Revolution

In the next few months everything was put on the back burner. Debussy didn't care if he missed homework assignments. He didn't care if he missed school. He didn't see any of his friends or his brother and mom, except at night. The spring would drift by and he wouldn't miss it. He borrowed a whole stack of Ho Goku books from Theodore and kept them under his bed with the other books from his dad's collection. Some were dialogues with world figures. Others were Buddhist history books. Still others were about the life philosophy of Nichiren's Buddhism. He also borrowed some of Ho Goku's books of poetry and his novelized history of the Buddhist lay organization, to which he was the third president-the "Society for the Creation of Value (SCV)," entitled *The Human Revolution.*

Debussy felt like a little kid opening Christmas presents. He couldn't wait to open each book and begin reading them. As he often did with other books, he skipped around from book to book. In *The Human Revolution* he learned that a school principal named Mr. Makiguchi and his successor, a schoolteacher named Mr. Toda originally founded the "Educational Society for the Creation of Value" (ESCV) in Japan in 1930, as an education society. Its main mission was to reform society, through first reforming the educational system of Japan. A few years before the founding of this society, Mr. Makiguchi wrote *The Value Creation Pedagogy,* which became the basis of the society's philosophy and teaching. Their goals were to inspire kids to use education as a means to become happy, and become positive assets to their communities. Their society consequently was comprised mainly of educators.

Mr. Makiguchi and Mr. Toda were introduced to the Buddhist philosophy of Nichiren, a 13th century Buddhist reformist, just two years before founding ESCV. Mr. Makiguchi's philosophy and Nichiren's Buddhism seemed to go hand in hand. They both empowered people to use their life for the sake of their own happiness, the happiness of others, and the betterment of society as a whole. Both stressed the importance of living in a mutually coexistent state with one's environment. They taught that in order to become happy, one must also contribute to the happiness of others. Buddhism calls this state of mutual coexistence or symbiosis "Dependent Origination."

As Ho Goku wrote in one of his poems,

Nothing in this world exists alone;
everything comes into being and continues
in response to causes and conditions.
Parent and child. Husband and wife.
Friend. Races. Humanity and Nature.
This profound understanding of coexistence, of symbiosis-
here is the source of resolution for the most pressing
and fundamental issues that confront humankind
in the chaotic last years of this century….

While these two great men were trying to raise a generation of youth that would contribute positively to society and the world, the Japanese military government was steering the country in the entirely opposite direction. As Mr. Makiguchi and Toda went head to head with the military establishment, they soon realized that their pedagogy would not be strong enough on its own to battle the state. Only the philosophy of Nichiren's Buddhism, based on the most powerful of all sutras, the "sutra of sutras," the "Sutra of the Wondrous Law of the Lotus Blossom" (or "Myo-ho Ren-ge Kyo," which is its Japanese/Chinese translation) would be mighty enough to do battle with the forces of darkness growing in Japan, leading up to World War II.

The forces of evil and the forces of good are often born together to do battle. It was no coincidence that the year 1928, the year the first two presidents of ESCV were introduced to Nichiren Buddhism, was also the same year a new high priest took control of the temple that claimed to be the true lineage of Nichiren's Buddhism. This high priest would eventually kowtow to the military establishment and enshrine the Shinto Talisman-the symbol of the military establishment's new state-mandated religion, completely abandoning the conviction and purity of Nichiren's Buddhism. This high priest would also admonish ESCV for not following the government.

There was also no coincidence that 1928 was the same year that both Ho Goku was born, and his later to-be, archrival, the illegitimate son of the high priest would be admitted into the priesthood at the young age of six. This illegitimate child-priest would later mussel his way to become high priest, and out of jealousy of ESCV's unprecedented growth throughout the world, under Ho Goku's leadership, would try to destroy ESCV and Ho Goku, its third president.

It was the same with Japan's military government. They came down hard on ESCV. Mr. Makiguchi and Toda were two strong antiwar, anti-state Shinto voices, who like Nichiren were heavily persecuted by the government for following their convictions. After much opposition, the government eventually imprisoned Mr. Makiguchi and Toda, along with some of the other leaders of the society. Unlike the other leaders however, Mr. Makiguchi and Toda held strong and never abandoned their faith and conviction. Mr. Makiguchi eventually died in prison. But after the war Mr. Toda emerged from prison and rebuilt the society, changing it from a society of educators to a Buddhist society for the common people. He dropped "Educational" from the title of the organization, and instead decided to call it, "Society for the Creation of Value (SCV)."

After the war the people of Japan were searching desperately to rebuild their nation, their communities, and their lives. They flocked in droves to SCV, and the promise the society provided, to not only change their karma, but also the karma of Japan, which had been ravaged by war. In those postwar days the society experienced phenomenal growth. The society became known by its critics as the "Society of the Sick and Poor." But as the members began invoking the power of "The Wondrous Law of the Lotus Blossom" in their lives, they began to drastically transform their lives. And soon, as the society grew from one sick old man released from prison to 10 million active members in Japan alone, Japan was transformed from a devastated island to a financial and industrial superpower. As the saying goes "the muddier the swamp, the more beautiful the lotus blossoms." Eventually, as the tides turned the members of the society began to be criticized by the authorities and the media for being too influential and too prosperous. What a great turn of fate-what a great human revolution.

Debussy managed to make it through the first semester unscathed. However he never gained the courage to talk to Lori all semester, even though he sat right next to her in history, and he had a locker two below hers. He chanted to somehow overcome his insecurity in talking to attractive girls. He could talk to any guy or for that matter any unattractive girl without hesitation or pause. Yet with the ones he was attracted to, he became all choked up and flustered. He chanted to once again have a class with Lori. They ended up in the same English class. He sat a little distance behind her, just as he had tried in history-just close enough to get a good view, yet not so close that she'd think anything of it.

Although he did gain a little confidence, the greatest thing he had gained from chanting over the last month was a sense of inner peace and the hope that everything would eventually change for the better. No matter how poor his family was, no matter how they had not been able to get out of that rundown apartment in the past, he somehow still had hope they soon would, if he kept chanting.

He was also more optimistic about the world now. The Gin"Grinch" puppets in Washington didn't manage in "one hundred days" to contract the people out as slaves as they had tried. They actually began to lose a little of their control over congress. But eventually Mr. Gin"Grinch" would be replaced by an equally destructive conservative Speaker of the House, Henry "Home Wrecker" Hyde-though this one wouldn't try to do as much to destroy the social safety net. Instead he would simply waste the taxpayers' money on a scandalous sexual impeachment process that would never fly, and would further weaken their parties control over congress.

Debussy was also encouraged by a movement, which he had kept his eyes on in the newspapers, which had been growing around the country and around the world. This was the people's movement to close "The Army School of The Americas" (SOA)-that notorious school in Georgia, whose graduates had been over and over implicated in human rights abuses around Central and South America.

As he had finished reading nine volumes of *The Human Revolution,* he proceeded to borrow *The New Human Revolution* from Theodore. The former was the novelized history of SCV under Presidents Makiguchi and Toda's leadership. And the latter was the novelized history of SCV under Ho Goku's leadership beginning in the 60's, as it moved from an organization of some one million members in Japan to become an organization that had over thirteen million members in over one hundred, ninety countries around the world. Since Ho Goku had not found anyone who could continue his novelized history as well as himself, he presented himself in the book using the fictitious name Shinichi Yamamoto.

As he contemplated the meaning of this growing people's movement to close SOA, he kept thinking of what Ho Goku had written in the first volume of *The New Human Revolution.*

> Nothing is stronger than the people. The power of the people is similar to the power of the Earth. Once the magma of the people's anger arises, tremors will follow with an energy that even moves mountains. One must never forget that the people are always the driving force for transforming society and the times.

This new movement to close SOA was, like most revolutionary movements, started by just one individual. This individual was Father Roy Bourgeois, a courageous Maryknoll priest who had been kicked out of Bolivia, "persona non grata," for trying to assist the poor. He was assigned there shortly after an SOA graduate and member of the SOA's "Wall of Fame" Hugo Banzer overthrew the democratically elected government and began targeting religious leaders who opposed his rule. However, he was much luckier than some of his fellow humanitarians working in Central and South America. For instance, he later found out that four churchwomen, whom he had worked with in the past, were killed by the Salvadorian Military for their human rights work. When he discovered men trained in America at SOA raped and killed these four churchwomen, he began a study of this School. He rented a small apartment across the street from ft. Benning, Georgia, where the school had been located since it was kicked out of Panama. He made his modest apartment into the office of what became the School of the Americas Watch (SOAW).

His research, with the assistance of others, uncovered some important facts. First, two thirds of those officers named in a UN Truth Commission Report on El Salvador for the worst atrocities committed during that country's brutal civil war were trained at SOA. For example:

Two of the three officers cited for assassinating Archbishop Oscar Romero “beloved champion of the poor,” while he celebrated mass were SOA trained.

All three members of the Salvadoran National Guard cited for the assassination of three labor union leaders at the Hotel Sheraton in San Salvador were SOA alumni.

Five linked to the case of the four raped and murdered churchwomen were SOA trained. Another was a guest speaker at the SOA. Two were granted residence in the US.

Nineteen of the twenty six cited for the massacre of six Jesuit priests, their housekeeper, and her teenage daughter at the priests’ residence at the University of Central America in San Salvador were SOA trained.

Ten of the twelve officers cited for the murder of 900 unarmed civilians, in what became known as the “El Mozote Massacre,” were SOA graduates-their bodies mutilated and burned or left to rot.

Outraged by all he knew, Father Roy couldn’t stay silent. He knew he must do something to stop this school from operating on $20 million of US taxpayers’ money each year. His first protest was a lone protest, but soon it would grow to thousands and thousands, until congress would be forced to cut the funding for this murderous institution, which protects American capitalism abroad.

His first protest was well planned out. He bought an officer’s uniform from an army surplus store down the street from the school. He took a boom box with a cassette tape of the late slain archbishop of El Salvador, Oscar Romero’s last sermon. This sermon was delivered the day before he was assassinated. It was a call to the military leaders of the country to stop the oppression of the people of El Salvador. This protest was held a day when many Salvadoran military men were being trained there, while they were in their barracks getting ready to go to sleep. He walked onto the base unimpeded. And as night fell, he climbed a tree next to their sleeping quarters and strung the boom box from a branch, and waited patiently until all lights were out. As the last light went out he pushed the play button, and the voice of Oscar Romero split the silence and awoke all in the barracks.

As the archbishop’s voice rang out, “In the name of the fathers of our country, in the name of god, I ask you to Please Stop The Oppression!” Soon searchlights went on and sirens blared, drowning out the martyr’s words. Father Roy was finally dragged from the tree and booked on charges of trespassing on federal property and impersonating an officer and was imprisoned.

As he says, "All good causes need someone in prison to ignite the movement." The next year he returned with a group of 10 to perform a vigil in front of the school, to commemorate the many Central and South Americans who have been brutalized, tortured, raped, and killed by SOA graduates over the decades. The ten also marched onto the school in a solemn funeral procession carrying wooden crosses baring the names of SOA victims and a black wooden casket. These 10 mothers, grandmothers, teachers, and pastors were all jailed for six months. This really ignited the movement. As Peter Gabriel sings "You can blow out a candle. But you can't blow out a fire. Once the flames begin to catch, the wind will blow it higher."

Once they were released they began traveling around the country lecturing at churches, universities, community centers, or in front of any group that was willing to listen to their story. Soon the group of ten grew to hundreds, then thousands.

It was an exponential growth from ten to over fifty, to over five hundred, to over two thousand, and finally to over seven thousand. The number of those at the protest who would risk arrest by marching over the line onto the base would continue growing, until last count some two thousand, three hundred people all carrying wooden crosses and some at the head of the procession carried black wooden caskets. Each year, until this time, everyone who crossed the line would get arrested and a heavy fine. However, once the protest grew to over two thousand entering the base, they didn't have enough military police to detain the protesters, so they were forced to simply escort them off the base and issue them warning letters.

At their first rally the ten were branded as "a ragtag bunch of wild-eyed hippies left over from the '60s." Now when over seven thousand people showed up to protest, the town mayor mingled with the crowd shaking hands. And Roy Bourgeois was awarded the Isaac Hecker Award for Social Justice.

One person dedicated to a worthwhile cause, who decides to take action, can change the fate of humanity. Debussy had hope that soon justice would prevail.

Julian

Debussy's second semester English class was proving to be the most enjoyable class he had. Not only was he glad to see Lori everyday, but he also found the young and progressive teacher, Ms. Baldwin to be a fresh breeze of change, compared with the conservative teachers he had in other classes. On a few occasions she even wore jeans to class. She was actually a student teacher, who was only supposed to substitute the class for a short time, while the older, permanent English teacher recovered from her winter illness. However, a few months had already passed, and there was no sign the elder teacher's condition was improving. It actually appeared to be getting worse.

Although the students who previously knew Mrs. Wilson hoped she was all right, no one wanted her to come back and replace Ms. Baldwin. Ms. Baldwin was in her late 20's. But she was so youthful that many students on campus often mistook her for one of the upper-class students.

To Debussy this seemed to be one of his first conspicuous results of chanting. One of the many things he chanted for when Theodore introduced him to *Nam Myo-ho Ren-ge Kyo* was to have a more enjoyable time at school, and to learn things that were legitimate-things, which would hopefully have some relevance to his life. He remembered reading Einstein say, "wisdom is what's left over when you forget everything you've learned in school." He hoped he wouldn't have to spend the next four years after high school trying to deprogram the erroneous conditioning he was being force-fed there. He also hated the constant tests he was given to see how well he could memorize the garbage the other teachers constantly filled him with.

He was impressed by Ms. Baldwin's enthusiasm, not only for teaching, but also for learning from the students. She opened up the class by introducing herself as the "temporary host of their journey into literature and a deeper grasp of the English language." She said as "host" she would journey into this subject with them, and hoped they would each discover things no one had yet discovered about the subject. She also said she hoped they would not only learn, but would teach her something new and exciting in the process. As Debussy believed school should be a place where people are taught how to learn and discover new things, not a place to be filled up with useless, superannuated misinformation. He felt students should be able to actively dispute in writing the information they were being presented with.

Instead of taking role call on the first day by calling out each person's name as it appeared on her printed roster-as other thoughtless teacher often do-she went around the room and let each student introduce themselves, and tell everyone how they would like to be addressed. She also asked each person to say one thing they liked most about himself or herself. Debussy was glad he would no longer be referred to as Mr. Jensen. He often thought last names were so redundant. "Why call a rose anything but a rose," as Shakespeare once wrote. Why call a dog, canis familiaris, or a cat, felis domestica, when you can simply call them dogs and cats. He hoped to be able to call Ms. Baldwin, Amy, as was her name. Of course, Debussy knew he didn't have to worry about any one confusing him with another "Debussy" on campus or another "Debut."

Ms. Baldwin was the first female on campus who got Debussy (if even for a moment) to take his eyes and attention off his obsession with Lori Thomson. She was a very in-shape lady with long strawberry blond hair and a light complexion, adorned with a small amount of freckles on her nose and cheeks, which she occasionally tried to cover up with a very light shade of make-up. She had a slight East Coast accent and a constant unaffected smile, which invited anyone to approach her. Although she had never married, she had a young five year old son, whom she had pictures of all over her desk. He was the apple of her eye.

As her turn came around for introductions, she picked up one of the pictures of her son and said, "What I like most about myself, is I gave birth to the most beautiful human being in the world. His name is Cole. I named him after Cole Porter, whose music I really enjoy." He had bright reddish-blond hair, and glowing blue eyes, with bushy red eyebrows.

Debussy had now been practicing Buddhism for some four months. And through his rigorous study in that time, he had become rather proficient in the philosophy of Nichiren's Buddhism and the Lotus Sutra, for someone so newly immersed in it. He wanted to share the feelings he was experiencing from the practice. However, he felt uncomfortable sharing it with his schoolmates. He felt they wouldn't be able to comprehend. But he was chanting to eventually be able to share it with this new teacher. She seemed very open minded. And he thought maybe he could introduce it to her through one of his writing assignments.

The first month they were given an assignment to find a novelist, and write an essay about that author, and one or more of his or her works. He searched for a novelist who wrote about Nichiren's Buddhism, but couldn't find one.

Debussy had been reading some of Gore Vidal's novels. He especially liked *Julian*, a historical novel about the 4th century Roman Emperor of the same name. He was particularly interested in Julian's attempts to keep the new "all embracing" religion of the "Galileans" from becoming the state-mandated religion. Although the Roman Empire was slowly crumbling, he felt this would not help it, but would rather do more harm than good. And as it turned out he was right. He also tried to preserve the various indigenous faiths of the Greeks, such as Hellenism.

Julian never lived to see the complete collapse of the empire. Yet as he feared the mixing of church and state not only proved to be a great cause of the empire's downfall, but also was responsible for the destruction and usurpation of Jesus' teachings along with that of the more traditional teachings. The new "all embracing" faith which was created by his uncle, the Emperor Constantine's haggling bishops bared little resemblance to the teachings of the Nazarene. In a slew of Ecumenical councils they invented the Trinity and removed reincarnation, a central teaching of Jesus from their new dogmatic teaching.

The second was hoped would make the people more loyal subjects to the mandates of the empire. It instead made people confused and apathetic about life. When everything in nature is constantly subject to the ongoing cycles of formation, continuance, decline, disintegration, and regeneration, it would seem bizarre to think somehow human life was the only life in the universe not subject to this natural flow. It would seem only obvious to any semi-enlightened society that if nature was subjected to certain laws of causation so to would human life, which is a product of nature. The many inconsistencies and contradictions they fabricated in their "New Book" left people helplessly confused. It was this confusion, which was one of the many causes for the downfall of Rome. The other was Rome's wars against the rest of the known world, which they referred to as barbarians. Empires can only hope to last so long, before their karma comes back to haunt them. Debussy knew the same fate would eventually return to the US Empire.

The Roman Empire so badly butchered the many books of James, Matthew, Timothy, John, Thomas and the rest, and left only segments that were in line with their political ideology. Anyone who taught any teachings that didn't agree with their "New Book" were summarily done away with or branded as heretics. To win converts to this new "all embracing" faith it was necessary to steal the teachings of all the other indigenous religions. As Debussy quoted Maximus, from Gore Vidal's novel in his essay:

> The Christians would impose one final rigid myth on what we know to be various and strange. No, not even myth, for the Nazarene existed as flesh while the gods we worship were never men; rather they are qualities and powers become poetry for our instruction. With the worship of the dead Jew, the poetry ceased.
>
> The Christians wish to replace our beautiful legends with the police record of a reforming Jewish rabbi. Out of this unlikely material they hope to make a final synthesis of all the religions ever known. They now appropriate our feast days. They transform local deities into saints. They borrow from our mystery rites, particularly those of Mithras. The priests of Mithras are called "father." So the Christians call their priest "fathers." They even imitate the tonsure, hoping to impress new converts with the familiar trappings of an older cult. Now they have started to call the Nazarene "savior" and "healer." Why? Because one of the most beloved of our gods is Asklepios, whom we call "savior" and "healer."....
>
> I betray no secret of Mithras when I tell you that we, too, partake of a symbolic meal. Recalling the words of the Persian prophet Zarathustra, who said to those who worshipped the One God-and Mithras, "He who eats of my body and drinks of my blood, so that he will be made one with me and I with him, the same shall know salvation." That was spoken six centuries before the birth of the Nazarene.

Debussy also quoted Priscus from the novel, explaining how these "Galileans" stole the date of December 25th (which had no relation to Jesus' birth, nor did the shepherds, which they claimed were at his side on that fabled day) and the Last Supper story from the Persian god, Mithras, and just about every other holiday or ceremony was ripped off from every ancient teaching known to the Western world. It's no wonder this "all embracing" church, has tried so desperately to keep the people ignorant of history. From the Dead Sea Scrolls, to Jesus' travels during the 17 lost years of his life, which they conveniently expunged from their history books.

Yet history goes on, with or without the tyrants who try to conceal it, and sooner or later people stumble upon the truth. Whether it's buried away in some boxes in someone's garage, or it's unknowingly stored on microfiche at the Huntington Library in Pasadena. They can burn the Library of Alexandria a million times and still truth will surface sooner or later.

As Priscus says in Gore Vidal's *Julian*:

> The Christians have slyly incorporated most of the popular elements of Mithras and Demeter and Dionysus into their own rites. Modern Christianity is an encyclopedia of traditional superstition.... Granted no educated man can accept the idea of a Jewish rebel as god. But having rejected that myth, how can one then believe that the Persian hero-god Mithras was born of light striking rock, on December 25th, with shepherds watching his birth? (I am told that the Christians have just added those shepherds to the birth of Jesus.)...Then Mithras is called up to heaven, after celebrating a sacramental last supper. Times end will be a day of judgment....
>
> Between the Mithraic story and its Christian sequel I see no essential difference. Admittedly the Mithraic code of conduct is more admirable than the Christian. Mithraists believe that right action is better than contemplation.... They were the first to teach that strength is gentleness. All of this is rather better than the Christian hysteria which vacillates between murder of heretics on the one hand and a cringing rejection of this world on the other. Nor can a Mithraist be absolved of sin by a sprinkle of water. Ethically, I find Mithras the best of all the mystery cults. But it is absurd to say it is any more "true" than its competitors. When one becomes absolute about myth and magic, the result can only be madness.

Which is exactly what occurred in Rome. As Debussy wrote in his essay, "How unfortunate that this madness has continued for two millennia." Someday people will be awoken from their delusion and know the real history. In his small way Debussy did all he could to add to that rude awakening, which was so needed-especially in Wutherington Beach, where madness was the life-style.

Debussy also used Gore Vidal's novel *Messiah*, and an extensive bibliography of other books to support his thesis. He quoted from *The Dead Sea Scrolls Deception, The Dark Years of Christian History, Reincarnation; The Phoenix Fire Mysteries, The Lost Years of Jesus, Holy Blood Holy Grail*, and a few other academic books on Gore Vidal.

Soon his paper grew from an essay to what could represent a college term paper. His chanting and study brought out a brilliant way to introduce Buddhism in his assignment. The more he studied the battle Julian waged with this new "Galilean" religion, the more he saw how there were many similarities with the battle Ho Goku was currently waging with the Nichiren Shoshu priesthood. The priesthood's decadence and deceit started coming to the surface under the direction of that illegitimate child priest, who was admitted into the priesthood the same year Ho Goku had been born, who now older was the high priest gone mad.

This priest, Nikken Abe was twisting the teaching of Nichiren to enhance his own power, much like Constantine's disgraceful bishops who completely distorted Christ's teachings for their own aggrandizement. However, Julian didn't care to save Christendom. He preferred the philosophy of Socrates to what he called, "the quarrels and intolerance of a sect whose purpose it is to overthrow that civilization whose first note was struck upon blind Homer's lyre." As he quoted Julian in his essay, from Gore Vidal's rendition of Julian's Memoir, "I learned that it is dangerous to side with any party of the Galileans, for they mean to overthrow and veil those things that are truly holy." He called their churches "Charnel Houses… a dig at their somewhat necrophile passion for the relics of dead men."

Although Julian was not trying to protect Jesus' teachings, the way Ho Goku and The SCV were fighting to save Nichiren's teachings, Debussy saw that the two battles, which these two great heroes were waging, were unprecedented historically. They were both waging courageous wars for truth and justice. Just as his contemporaries had labeled Julian the "Apostate," Ho Goku was constantly bashed in the Japanese periodicals of yellow journalism, as the "Billion-Dollar Cult Leader," who wished to "rule all of Japan." Even the US trash media, Hard Copy played some bogus stories about him.

However, Ho Goku didn't let these unfounded, puerile attacks, from the meager minds of an island nation stop his quest to fight for what he knew was right and just. Although Julian was not successful in stopping the "Galileans," Ho Goku rallied the millions of bodhisattvas who were emerging from the Earth, just as predicted in the Lotus Sutra, in a time Buddhism called the "Latter Day of the Law."

The early Christian movement was, like the SCV, a movement of the common people. So the Roman Empire believed that by hijacking the Christian's mascot for their own "all embracing" creation, they would be able to keep the masses under their control. Too bad the early movement of the "Galileans" wasn't led by a great leader of the common people, like SCV was. If only the peasants of Rome would have rose up against their crooked Bishops the way SCV rose up against the malevolent high priest, Nikken and his megalomaniacal men in robes, the correct teachings of Christ would maybe be taught today. But then again the Roman government was way more repressive to nonconformists than Japan's in the 1900's. The 4th century Roman government burned, butchered, and hung those who didn't obey their dictates.

Debussy felt very akin with Julian. Both had lost their fathers at an early age. Julian's father was taken away and killed on orders from his own family, the new Emperor of Rome, Constantius, shortly after Julian's uncle and former Emperor, Constantine had passed away. Julian was six years old at the time. However unlike Debussy, Julian also lost his mother at birth.

As Debussy read about Julian's early childhood and adolescence, he could relate well with the anger Julian felt toward everything. A boy can feel disconnected with life without a father or mother. Often they feel they don't belong to the world. They feel they are but half a person. How much worse would it be he wondered, to have neither parent? As he read about Julian's memories of his father, he recalled once again those few memories he still had of his own father. Or was it only one memory? He only had one picture of Charles Xanthankis. It was one of his parents' wedding pictures. Or was it the only one they ever took? He had seen it but a few times; it was kept in a shoebox with a bunch of old photos of Zeus and himself, when they were babies. There were no pictures of his father around the house.

Like Debussy, Julian had been a shy boy who spent most of his childhood engulfed in books and daydreaming. Also despite Julian's anger and pessimism toward the world, he was a very compassionate person who by some stroke of luck, fate, or fortune managed to rise up to become the Emperor of Rome. Debussy always had some strange inner feeling he too would be a great leader someday. The story of Julian's life, despite its early tragedies, gave Debussy a sense of hope that his life too would soon change for the better. Debussy like Julian didn't desire fame or fortune; he simply wanted to serve humanity in a positive way.

When he finally turned in his long paper, he was elated that his teacher gave him an "A minus." However, he was so disgusted by how the other classes were being taught that he barely managed to pass his first semester with a low "C minus" average. Ms. Baldwin wrote comments on his paper before returning it, about how she enjoyed his writing style and insight. As she put it, he should "keep writing; you have power with words." It was exactly the boost he needed.

Debussy knew if anyone had the potential to write, then we all have the latent potential to do so. The trick was to manifest that latent potential. As he chanted he slowly was able to tap into his innate wisdom. He remembered reading Thomas Edison say, "genius is one percent inspiration, and ninety-nine percent perspiration." The reason most people fail to accomplish anything great, is not because they don't possess the latent genius. It's because they never manifest their geniusness, which Buddhism calls "Buddhahood." They simply fail to take the repeated actions over and over, again and again, without ever giving up, which would allow them to eventually tap into their true and unlimited potential. As Debussy was learning, this is the only thing that separated a "winner" from a "loser." If one never gives up, one can never fail to win. When faced with difficulties, it is the person who has jumped the most hurdles and broke down the most walls who will create something truly inspirational.

Zeus

Debussy was sitting in his bedroom reading one of the letters, which Nichiren wrote to one of his followers, when suddenly Zeus busted into the room. "What up, punk?"

"Nothing. Just readin'." Debussy replied dryly.

"What are you fuckin' talking about? It's Saturday night! What do you mean, *you're just readin'?*"

"That's it. Saturday, Sunday, Monday-it makes no difference to me. Morning turns to afternoon, then turns to night. It's all the same. No better time than now to read."

"What are you turning into some brainiac, fuckin' reading all the time? Nathan and Christopher have been askin' about you. I told them you've probably been home jackin' off. I told them that me and mom haven't seen much of you lately either." He turned on some loud punk rock music. Debussy had almost forgotten about the Dead Kennedy's, and the other punk bands he too used to blare so loudly. For some reason since he'd been chanting that screaming hadn't appealed to him as much anymore. And now as it was disturbing his reading, he became extremely annoyed by it.

"Why don't you turn that crap off? I'm tryin' to fuckin' read!"

"What have you gone mad? This is the fuckin' Dead Kennedy's!" Zeus began circling around the room swinging his clenched fist in circles around his head, while belting out the lyrics:

"So you've been to school for a year or two.
and you think you've seen it all?
In daddy's car thinkin' you'll go far.
Back East your type don't crawl."

Each time he circled by Debussy's bed, he would either kick Debussy's foot or leg with his steel toe boots.

"Playin' ethnic jazz to parade your snazz
on your five grand stereo.
Braggin' that you know how the niggers feel cold
and the slums got so much soul."

Finally Debussy picked up a shoe and heaved it at Zeus's back. Eventually if Zeus kept it up Debussy would throw something at his head.

To protect himself against Zeus and Zeus's best friend, Adrian's constant abuse, he developed a pretty good throwing arm. And when they got him angry enough he was likely to throw anything he could pick up-a chair, a rock. It was his only defense against these two.

***

One time in the kitchen Zeus socked Debussy in the arm. So Debussy picked up the first thing he could get his hands on. It was an orange from the fruit basket on the kitchen counter. He heaved it at Zeus's head. Luckily, Zeus managed to duck in time. Unlucky for them both, however, it went straight through both kitchen windows, which were open upon each other. Needless to say, Justine was quite upset at both of them. They had to board those windows up for several months, before she scraped up enough money to finally fix them.

They still had a big hole in their bedroom wall, where Zeus and Adrian were wrestling with Debussy, and Zeus's boot had smashed into it. He was practicing one of his rolling judo flips on Debussy. However, Debussy's strong grip on the back of Zeus's pants and studded belt caused him to flip along with Debussy.

***

Debussy finally got up and turned off the stereo, as Zeus was screaming out the lyrics and dancing around the room. This didn't stop Zeus however.

"It's time to taste what you must fear.
Right Guard will not help you here.
It's a holiday in Cambodia.
It's tough kid but it's life.
It's a holiday in Cambodia.
Don't forget to pack a wife."

As he broke into the chorus, he began to swing both his arms with clenched fists, and kick out both of his legs, storming straight into Debussy, who tried to circle away from him. He knocked Debussy into the dresser. This angered Debussy, so Debussy started swinging his arms and legs and began slamming into Zeus. They formed a perfect two-man mosh pit, until Debussy's body slammed Zeus into the stereo, causing it to drop off the table between their beds. It was a pretty old, rundown stereo. This could have likely been its last blow. Finally Zeus wrestled Debussy to the floor and got him in a headlock.

Justine heard the loud noise and came to the door yelling. "What's going on in there?" She opened the door and started yelling at Zeus to get off of Debussy. She nudged him lightly on the side with her foot. "Come on. Get off him! What's going on in here?"

"Debussy turned off the stereo. Then he knocked me into it."

"Shut up you jack ass, you started punching and kicking at me. I was just protecting myself."

"Debussy! Stop using that language! And Zeus! Get out of here! Debussy was minding his own business till you came barging in on him. Go out and do something with your friends." She was always getting mad at them for going out all day and night with their friends. But as soon as they were home for longer than an hour together, they got on her nerves. And finally she would order one or both to leave the house.

Zeus got up, brushed himself off, and walked out saying, "Fuckin' sissy!"

"Zeus!" Justine pushed him on the shoulder out of the room. Debussy picked up the stereo. The cassette drawer was hanging on by one side. He pushed it in.

"So what's up? How come you haven't been goin' out with your friends lately?" Justine asked, with a concerned look on her face.

"You never liked us goin' out late before. How come you'd all of a sudden care now?"

"You've just been acting strange lately. Is there something wrong?"

"High school's different. I'm no longer a little kid. My old junior high friends just seem to be playin' like they're still in junior high. It seems like a big waste of time to me."

"I fear you're getting more and more like your father everyday."

They both paused for a moment and stared at each other blankly. Was she going to actually talk about Charles? Debussy never recalled her bringing up his name in a conversation. So he sat and waited. But she too remained mute.

Eventually she broke the silence, but changed the subject. "I got offered a job yesterday."

"I've been hoping you would."

"What would make you think about me getting a different job? I've been working in the same line of work for as long as I can remember."

"Just a feeling I've had." He sat there silent for a moment then nervously asked, "Do you remember dad chanting 'Nam Myo-ho Ren-ge Kyo?'" He had never asked her anything about his father.

"Where did you hear that?"

"What do you know about it?" Debussy, playing politician, often answered her questions with other questions, throwing her off guard.

"Along with his many other chants, 'Na-Mu Amidha Butsu,' his 'Hue' chants, his various ancient Judaic chants in Latin, or whatever language it was, and his millions of different meditations, he would throw in that phrase a few times. He tried everything he could. Nothing kept him out of trouble with the law and the government though. He was always out trying to save the world. But, he could fuc' (she almost said fucking, but stopped herself) barely save his damn marriage. His dying is the only thing that kept us from getting a divorce." She started getting really emotional. It was amazing how mention of that one small phrase, which made Debussy feel so great, could spark such memories in Justine. Tears started to come to her eyes.

***

Debussy had never seen her cry about his father. At least he never expected her crying to be related in any way to him. She did cry often. He never knew what it was she was crying about. He just figured it was a thing women do. Often she would drink Japanese, Akadama plum wine, while she cleaned the house on the weekends, and blare David Bowie music so loudly, the whole neighborhood could hear. After cleaning she would lock herself in the bathroom and cry in a hot bath. At that point she was too drunk to notice her sobs were being heard outside the bathroom, even over the running water and loud music.

It was usually only Debussy who stayed home while she cleaned. Not having a father, Debussy often fantasized that David Bowie was his dad. His mom had so many posters of him around the house and no pictures of her deceased husband. Debussy would sing along to every song as she cleaned. And eventually he would be knocking at the bathroom door asking her what was wrong. She always said “nothing. I’m just sad.”

He would often persist, asking her “about what?”

She always recited the same lines: “Oh it’s nothing. I just feel like crying sometimes.” He would sit there listening to her, and eventually start crying himself. It was a confusing feeling; he was crying because he was sad that she was sad. Yet he knew not what she was sad about. Over the years crying came quite naturally to him. He could cry on the slightest thought of sadness. Sometimes he would walk home from school, and as he got closer to his cockroach-infested apartment he would start crying. He wouldn’t know why; he just figured he was crying like his mother; because he felt like it.

When he first started smoking pot at age twelve, he thought it would help him not feel like crying. Although he laughed a lot during the high, once the temporary elation evaporated, it only made him feel emptier. When he first started chanting it was as if a trickling dam that had leaked for many years suddenly burst. However, for once he was crying tears of joy. Over the last couple of months he had been chanting much more about his mother than himself. He wanted her to smile and mean it. He wanted to feel her happiness.

Although he had a crush on Lori Thompson, his extreme love for his mom, the only woman in his life was beyond anything he could feel for some young girl at school. As Freud argued, a young boy's first love is often his mother. Debussy was the perfect example of Freud's theory. He would often secretly peer through the crack in the doorway of her room as she dressed, and be spellbound by her beauty and voluptuousness.

He would also sit next to her on the couch after she took her drunken bath, and watch her as she fell asleep in only a wet towel, which would often reveal most of her naked body. He would pretend to be reading, but as she drifted off, he would look over his book and fantasize caressing her wet, naked body.

***

Now Debussy hugged her tightly as she began to cry. He asked softly, "How did dad die?" Her breasts were poking his chest through her light blouse, as her chest heaved up and down.

Through the sobs she whispered. "I don't know. He was involved in so many things. He was fighting for every social struggle around the world. 'Saving the world from US imperialism.' He would always say. He for a while got involved with the Symbionese Liberation Army, and even with the Black Panthers, and every damn peasant movement from Mexico to Chile. He was doing radio programs, which brought to light the US involvement in these countries. Many times, we could tell we had our phones bugged. Sometimes people would call up and start asking questions about him, and would not identify themselves. I occasionally saw strange cars with suited men, watching outside our house. That's why I changed our name and moved as soon as he passed away.

"He's lucky he didn't get us all killed, when he went down to El Salvador the last time. I didn't even want to say 'good bye.' I had an eerie feeling he wouldn't come back. He was such a fanatic about everything."

Debussy sat and pondered this last line. For a while he had become quite a fanatic, while reading his dad's books. Luckily Theodore had been teaching him what Buddhism called "The Middle Way." It was important to find balance in everything. Life was a constant balancing act. Fortunately Debussy was learning this lesson at such a young age. As he held his mother, he chanted silently to himself hoping the “Wondrous Law of the Lotus Blossom” would penetrate through his mother’s sadness. “Nam Myo-ho Ren-ge Kyo, Nam Myo-ho Ren-ge Kyo, Nam Myo-ho Ren-ge Kyo.”

Nichiren

It was through Ms. Baldwin's encouragement that Debussy eventually came to find what it was he wanted to devote his life to. His mission he felt was to effect a positive change in the world by becoming a writer. It's quite extraordinary the amount of influence an adult's encouragement can have on shaping a young person's life. Even just a few words of support can change its entire course. Debussy knew that through chanting and never giving up he would eventually be a great writer. He was so fascinated by Gore Vidal's two historical novels, *Julian* and *Lincoln* that he decided he would start his writing career by writing an historical novel himself.

To his knowledge, no one had yet written a novel exclusively about the life of Nichiren. Although the life of both Emperor Julian and Abraham Lincoln were eventful, they paled in comparison with the life of this 13th century Buddhist revolutionary. He decided then that he would spend his spare time studying Nichiren's life, his many writings, and the history of 13th century Kamakura, Japan, where Nichiren spent much of his time teaching the populace. He made it his goal to finish the novel by the time he finished high school.

Debussy learned that Nichiren, like Jesus, was persecuted by the authorities for his religious convictions. Unlike Jesus however, Nichiren managed to escape death on numerous occasions. One of the most miraculous occasions was undoubtedly the night he was taken down to the beach at Tatsunokuchi, on orders from the government. He was scheduled to be beheaded there shortly before dawn. His executioner and a group of soldiers escorted him on horseback in the dead of the night. On route to the beach, he summoned one of his most courageous successors, the young samurai named Shijo Kingo and the four Shijo Brothers, who all lived nearby. The young Kingo was so loyal to his mentor that he vowed to die alongside him. He clung to the reigns of Nichiren's horse and refused to let go. He stood by Nichiren to the last, as mentor and successor; they were as inseparable as an image and its shadow, even in the face of death. Nichiren stayed strong in his conviction, and unshakenly vowed to die upholding his faith.

Shortly before he was to be beheaded, Shijo Kingo began to weep. Nichiren however admonished him by saying, "to be able to die for the Lotus Sutra is the greatest honor." However, before the executioner could raise his sword, a blinding orb pierced the night sky.

Debussy later learned while reading the dialogue entitled *Buddhism and the Cosmos* that this fateful night occurred during a time in which Haley's Comet was closest to the Earth's atmosphere. This glowing object, which shot through the sky, is now believed by researchers to have possibly been caused by some large piece of debris from the comet, which may have skimmed the Earth's atmosphere. "Too bad no comet streaked by Golgotha 2000 years ago. Perhaps history would be quite different." Debussy thought to himself.

Whatever the case was, the executioner dropped to his knees and a few soldiers ran off, while others began bowing their heads and praying to Nichiren. Nichiren replied by scolding the executioner to proceed with the execution and not be such a coward. He demanded "you must kill me now while it's still dark. Because by morning it will be too ugly a job." Instead the executioner shrunk back in fear. Later, on their return from the execution site, Nichiren ordered sake be served to the soldiers, many of whom decided to take faith in his teachings.

***

The job Justine was offered ended up being out in the valley. Since her old car wouldn't hold up the long drive everyday, if she were to take the job, they would have to move inland. She was very concerned how Debussy would feel about transferring schools right after his freshman year. However, the new job would be making her considerably more money, and for the first time she would only have to work one job. To top it off she would finally be able to move them into a house.

Actually this was just what Debussy had been chanting for. He was sick of his old friends anyhow. He was always looking for excuses of how he could keep from having to smoke out with them. The excuses were beginning to run out. He also didn't care much for his school nor the teachers, except Ms. Baldwin of course. But then again, who knew, soon, the old teacher would eventually replace her. He knew something this good couldn't last forever.

From Theodore's guidance, and from his study of Nichiren's writings, Debussy was learning to embrace change. After all, everything in the universe is in a constant state of flux. If we try to build our happiness on things that are by their very nature transient, we will only be led to misery, when the winds of change begin to blow our way. The only unchangeable reality is the law of life itself, or as Buddhism calls it, Nam Myo-ho Ren-ge Kyo-that ultimate unchangeable reality that underlies all change-in a sense a universal consciousness, or as Buddhism also calls it, the "Ninth Level of Consciousness."

When one bases one's happiness on this fundamental law of life, one learns to look forward to things always constantly changing for the better. When one bases their happiness on the force of life that is "even greater than the strength of nuclear weapons," as Ho Goku wrote, there is no amount of change that can keep one from manifesting a sense of joy for living, even in the face of tremendous adversity. When one becomes in rhythm with the forces of change in the universe, all change inevitably moves them in the direction toward fulfillment and happiness.

Debussy read in one of Nichiren's letters to the samurai, Shijo Kingo that "worthy persons deserve to be called so because they are not carried away by the eight winds: prosperity, decline, disgrace, honor, praise, censure, suffering, or pleasure. They are neither elated by prosperity nor grieved by decline." This from a person who was in exile on the ice covered, Sado Island for his beliefs. While in exile he claimed he was the happiest man in all of Japan. The more people persecuted him, he asserted, the happier he became. For this proved the prophesies in the Lotus Sutra that states, one who attempts to practice this pure teaching in a defiled age will be met with persecution after persecution. Such persons, regardless of any change of circumstance, will not lose their inner state of peace and confidence in their own power to direct their destiny forward for the better. The 'eight winds' are simply a brief representation of all changes that can occur in one's life, whether good or bad, which weak-willed people often get swept away by.

Staying true to yourself and staying strong whether things are going good or bad is the key to a Buddhist practice, as Debussy was learning. Nichiren was the greatest example of this forbearance. As other religions try to assert control over other people, Buddhism teaches one how to control oneself, which is far more difficult and far more important. Regardless of what happens in life, the incidents are neither positive nor negative; they are all relative to how one reacts to them.

Circumstances are only positive or negative, good or bad depending on how one chooses to respond to the situation. One's response is the sole determinate of the outcome. From no situation, regardless of how negative it may appear on the surface, can one not learn and grow.

Now Debussy felt his family's move could bring him new exciting changes and new possibilities. He chanted he would move into the best neighborhood, meet the best friends, and go to the best school, with the best teachers. He didn't share what he was chanting for with anyone. He just wrote down all his goals in a notebook and kept it under his bed, reading it and adding to it every time he chanted. In this way he was in a sense willing into being the future changes he wished to see. He was not praying as some do, "begging for favorable circumstances." He was instead pledging to create the life he wanted and he deserved, and that he had the unlimited power to create.

"Hey Debussy?" Christopher came running across the street to Lake Park.

Debussy hadn't walked home with him or Nathan in quite a while. So this unexpected voice from behind startled him somewhat. He turned around and exclaimed, "Hey Chris! How you doin' man?"

"Pretty Cool. Where you been? Nathan has been saying all kinds of crap about you lately. He said you've 'probably been home whacking it for the last few months.'"

"I guess he's the authority on whacking it, so he'd know. That's all right; he can take away my negative karma. I've got lots to expiate." Debussy didn't at all seem phased by the news of Nathan ripping on him. He felt it was a sign of Nathan's lack of self-esteem. When someone has to say bad things about another person, it's usually because they dislike their own self. And they are trying to make others feel as insignificant as they feel.

"How come I haven't seen you walking home lately? God I don't even have any classes with you this semester. I have that prick you had last semester though. You know, Mr. 'Crap-ton!'"

"Damn, you guys call him that too?" Although Debussy hadn't thought of Christopher for a while, he suddenly felt he missed him.

Christopher continued, "I haven't even seen you around school lately."

"Oh I've been hangin' low. And I've been goin' to the library after school lately. I just haven't felt like smokin' out or anything."

"Yeah me neither." Christopher looked down cast as he said it.

"Well then why don't you stop?" Christopher seemed a little hurt by this question, and taken aback. But that wasn't Debussy's intention. Christopher never asked himself why he kept smoking out with Nathan. He felt he had to, in order to be accepted hanging out with him and the others. Also Nathan often tried to force him if he refused, or at least made him feel guilty. Debussy said it more out of compassion. To act compassionately to your friends, sometimes you have to say things to them that may hurt their feelings. Things that hopefully will make them think.

While Christopher was searching for an answer, Debussy jumped back in, "I can see why someone might have wanted to hang out with Nathan in junior high school. We were thought to be cool back then, 'cause we were considered the class clowns. No one gives a rat's ass about that now. No one's considered cool in high school-at least not by the majority. Maybe some small clique considers someone cool, but everyone else thinks they're a complete jerk, regardless of who they are, or what they do. If you're not a jock, one tenth of the school thinks you're a dickhead. If you're not a bando, you can't hang around the music department, without getting strange looks. If you don't have your hair down to your knees, don't expect the Heshers to give you the time of day. If you're not a wanna-be gangster, don't try hangin' around behind the quad. If you don't smoke cigarettes, fuck trying to be a partier. If you don't got glasses, don't try to get in Chess Club, or the Academic Decathlon.

"High school is *so* lame that way. Who would want to try to be different? It's more different to try to be normal. Who would care to be accepted? No one can accept anything; they can't even accept themselves; 'cause they can't stand themselves. So everyday they are wasting their time, trying to change what they were yesterday. And soon they will try to change that; cause no one cares about them; cause they don't even give a shit about their own self.

"It used to appear cool to wear earrings back in junior high, and spike our hair up; 'cause no one else did that. And that was considered different from the norm. Now everyone's trying to be different. The more they try, the trendier they appear. Now you got to not only have your ear pierced to look cool. But you got to get your damn nose pierced, your eyebrow pierced, your lip pierced, your fuckin' tongue, nipple, clit, dick, and any other part of your body pierced you can imagine. I wouldn't be surprised if everyone started dying from heavy metal poisoning, with all that crap sticking through them. I saw this one goofball who looked like Frankenstein with some fuckin' metal thing stickin' out of his neck.

"Then you got to get something stupid tattooed on you, or you're not 'in style.' What are they gonna do when it starts to be the 'in-thing' to not have tattoos? Are they gonna start tryin' to remove them like the Sneetches in Doctor Seuss's book, with the stars on their bellies? I swear high school seems like such a joke. I try to stay away from it as much as possible. The only cool teacher I've had is a sub. Of course she's not permanent. Nothin's permanent in high school. One day you got to wear a Mohawk, the next everyone will be wearing their hair like freakin' Alfalfa. I thought we were supposed to act more mature in high school?"

Christopher didn't know what to say to all of this. He never thought about it. He was always trying so hard to be accepted. He didn't think to wonder why. Now he felt a little embarrassed by the whole thing. Sensing his discomfort, Debussy said, "Well I think we're all victims of societal pressures. I wish it were easier to just be ourselves, and not put on so many fronts. I'm sure you too wished people would accept you for who you are." He quickly dropped the subject, not wanting to make his friend feel too uncomfortable. He knew his friend wouldn't be able to change the circumstances at school. And he knew Christopher was just playing the part of a leaf blowing in the wind; he would drift any way people wanted to blow him. Debussy could only feel sorry for him, and hope to someday influence him to change.

The more Debussy thought about it, the more he saw how these separate cliques continued after high school. He saw grown adults, who put people down, who are different from them, were no better than adolescents. He saw how the people in governments were still not grown up, when they were trying to paint leaders of other countries as bad, simply because they were different. Debussy thought the whole idea of people trying to be different seemed so juvenile. And he wished the leaders of the world would some day grow up, and see that we are all human. He read in one of Ho Goku's poems that this fragmenting of people, who appear different on the surface, is the root of most of the problems facing humanity. In a poem to the Los Angeles members Ho Goku wrote:

> As each group seeks their separate roots and origins,
> society fractures along a thousand fissure lines.
> When neighbors distance themselves from neighbors,
> continue your uncompromising quest for your truer roots
> in the deepest regions of your lives.
> Seek out the primordial "roots" of humankind.
> Then you will without fail discover the stately expanse of *jiyu*
> unfolding in the depths of your lives.
>
> Here is the home, the dwelling place to which humankind
> traces its original existence-beyond all borders,
> beyond all differences of gender and race.
> Here is a world offering true proof of our humanity.
> If one reaches back to these fundamental roots,

all become friends and comrades.
To realize this is to "Emerge from the Earth."

Jiyu is the Japanese word for "freedom," which is the true state of a "Bodhisattva of the Earth." A Bodhisattva is someone who realizes that at the core of their life exists the state of compassion, and they work to bring out that natural state. And in so doing they become truly "human."

Debussy and Christopher walked through the park on their old route home. However, they cut through some alleys, instead of walking walls. Spring was in full bloom, and summer was just around the corner. They both strolled along thinking about the way it used to be-about last summer. Neither said much, but they both had smiles on their faces. Yeah pretty soon they'd be out of school. And they'd spend all summer at the beach again.

At that thought, suddenly Debussy remembered he'd be moving inland. And it may be harder for him to get to the beach. "So did you hear my mom got a job inland? And we're gonna be moving into a new house there."

"Yeah, I heard Zeus mention something about that to Adrian the other night. I hear Zeus's gonna spend his last year at Adrian's house, on the weeknights, so he can finish at Wutherington Beach. What are you gonna do?"

He hadn't thought that all of a sudden he'd feel as he did now. He was happy about the move before. But now he already started to miss Wutherington Beach. And he wasn't even leaving for a couple of months. Although it was fairly warm out all day, he unexpectedly felt a slight chill blow over him. He saw the cathedral ceilings of his school-the bell tower-everything flashed though his mind. Although there were things he didn't like about his town, he had come to the realization that there was so much he had taken for granted, which was so pleasant.

Now he didn't want to get home and read his books. He wanted that walk home to last forever. He longed to hear the chimes ring out, and the helicopter circle over head, and the squeaking sound of the old oil wells, teeter tottering up and down. Suddenly Hidden Valley came to his mind-the underground clubhouse. The tall trees he'd climb by the pond. The bike tracks they'd dug in the side of the hills. It all flashed though his mind. "Hey how's the club house doing?" He asked Christopher, with a look of excitement, hoping perhaps they could go there today.

"Shit you didn't hear?" Christopher said with a disturbed look on his face. "The cops found it. Had it bulldozed over."

His heart sank. He felt a dagger going through his chest. He felt he could cry. Yet he held back the tears, on his friend's behalf. They both walked in silence for a moment. Debussy pictured the three of them laughing in their chairs, their candles flickering. He wasn't however mad at the police. It served him right he felt. How could he just take it all for granted? He wished he'd spent more time there that year. Now he could never again.

Christopher tried to soften the blow, "Well shit man, we can always build another one, somewhere else?"

Debussy didn't reply. He looked up to the sky. There was a slight cloud cover rolling in. He felt it was going to blanket his heart and the anguish he felt.

Christopher interrupted his contemplation, "You want to come over and hang out at my house? My parents aren't gonna be home till real late."

"Alright." Debussy wasn't going to be stupid and miss any more moments in Wutherington Beach, if he could help it.

Planting the Seed

As they sat on a couch in Christopher's living room, Debussy glanced around at the spacious interior of Christopher's house. It was so big to him. "Imagine living in a house with two floors," he thought to himself. He fantasized getting up in the morning, walking down the stairs, and making some hot tea. It wasn't the nicest house in town. But to Debussy, next to Theodore's it was the best he'd ever been in. He wasn't much into material things. But he thought it sure would be great to live in a little better place than his, without cockroaches everywhere, at least. Having a room of his own would be nice too.

As he was peering around the house a cat rubbed up against his leg. He bent down to pet it. It was a very friendly and fluffy calico cat, with a big bushy tail. It seemed to call out to Debussy to pick it up.

They weren't allowed to have pets in Debussy's apartment, but occasionally the strays would sleep on his covered porch, at the top of the stairs, on his doormat, trying to avoid the cold.

He picked up the cat, sat it on his legs, as he made himself at home.

"That's Whiskers. He loves everyone who will pet him. He'll purr for hours. Do you want anything to munch on?" Christopher was rummaging through the pantry for food.

Debussy was glad he asked. He was used to feeling a little hungry after school. He usually didn't have that much money for lunch, to get enough to fill himself up completely. After school, he would be lucky if he could find something at his house with which to possibly make a peanut butter and jelly sandwich, or maybe some noodle soup. He occasionally found some popping corn to put in the air popper.

I guess that is why it was so easy for him to justify shop lifting in the past. He also got so hungry at the beach during summer that he would steal people's wallets off their towel. He wouldn't take everything that was in the wallet, just the money. But now that Theodore had been teaching him about the law of cause and effect, he couldn't rationalize making the causes anymore to further worsen his financial karma.

It's amazing that although he'd been chanting less than six months, he stopped shoplifting and stealing things, and he'd already seen his family's financial karma improve somewhat. Or at least it was scheduled to improve with Justine's new job.

He glanced over at Christopher and noticed the pantry was full of food-everything one could think of. To Debussy, it looked like a miniature grocery store. He could see why Christopher wasn't as interested in shoplifting as Nathan and he was. Christopher didn't need to steal food, when he had a house full of it.

"Sure I'll have one of those granola bars"-Debussy's mouth watering.

Christopher brought a few different kinds, and they ate them while catching up on old times. Debussy was so surprised how different Christopher seemed to him. "Did Christopher change? Or was it me who had changed?" Debussy thought to himself. Theodore had told Debussy that if someone changes their basic life-state everything and everyone in their environment would change. The individual and their environment are definitely interconnected. A change in one person's life, like a pebble dropped on the surface of a lake sends ripple effects throughout the entire lake and all feel the change, even if only on a subconscious level.

So many things happen subconsciously. Debussy was learning in Buddhism about the levels of consciousness, below even the storage of information level, which Western science calls the subconscious. Below this is a level of consciousness that is a reservoir of all the actions taken in the past, whether positive or negative. This is the storehouse of karma. Karma is an Indian word meaning action. The actions, whether they are thoughts, words, or deeds are forever recorded, and like a magnetic energy, they draw into a person's life a similar reaction from the environment.

Debussy could see by Christopher's financial circumstance that he had obviously made more positive causes in this life and in past lives in relationship to finances, than either Debussy or Nathan. And it was also apparent in his tendencies in the present. He was far more reluctant to steal than the others were. And if it weren't for meeting them, he would never have stolen a thing.

The great thing is that karma is entirely mutable. Regardless of the actions one has taken in the past, anyone can begin making new karma, by taking different actions now. With this realization, Debussy tried not feeling jealous by what Christopher had, which he didn't. Instead he made a determination that he would change his karma, so he could reap the same benefits in the future.

Now that he was relating to Christopher in a way he had never done in the past, he could see so much deeper into Christopher's life.

He saw that even though he lived in a nice house and had many luxuries, which Debussy could only dream of having, he was very sad, and didn't feel good about himself. He was always wanting to be like his friend Nathan, who didn't have the financial resources, but was at one time more popular. Even though Nathan was no longer popular like he was in junior high, Christopher clung to the concept of Nathan being the class clown, whom everyone wanted to hang around. Yet in high school, besides Christopher, there were few who cared to hang around him.

Debussy wanted Christopher to feel the sense of self worth, confidence, and appreciation, which he was now feeling, since he had started chanting. He knew it might be hard to introduce chanting to his friend, if he told him it was Buddhism. So he tried his best to relate it to Christopher in a way he may be able to accept it. "Have you seen that Tina Turner movie, 'What's Love Got To Do With It'?"

"Yeah. I saw some of it. My dad and mom rented it once. I didn't watch it all though. Was it good?"

"Well in that movie she chants, 'Nam Myo-ho Ren-ge Kyo,' and I've been trying it too."

"You been what? Is that a song?" Christopher was perplexed.

"It's a chant. You just say, 'Nam Myo-ho Ren-ge Kyo.'" Debussy said it slower this time.

Now even more confused Christopher laughed, "Why would you do that?"

"It makes me feel really good inside. Watch try saying it."

Christopher was so used to going along with whatever his friends asked him to try that he just went along. "What was it again?"

"Say, 'Nam,' like in Vietnam."

"Nam." Christopher tried copying him slowly. And he did it OK.

"Now say 'Myo.' Almost like a cat says, 'meow,' but instead of an 'awe' sound at the end say, 'Yo,' like 'me-Yo.' But with a shorter 'E' sound."

Christopher started laughing again, and with a low voice, he said, "Hey Yo! Me Yo!"

Debussy laughed along with him. He knew it would be strange for his friend to hear this for the first time. But he went on anyway. "Now say, 'Ho,' just like Santa Claus says, 'ho ho ho.'"

"Ho." He continued laughing, "Now what is this?"

"Oh just try it. Now say, 'Ren,' like Wren and Stimpy."

"OK, Ren." He said, giggling slightly.

"Now say, 'Ge' like you're queer."

"What?" Christopher was rolling now.

"Ge, like 'gay.'"

"Dude that's gay."

"No just trust me, you'll be glad you can say it." Debussy couldn't control his laughter either, but he tried to contain himself and go on. "OK now say 'Kyo' like Tokyo."

"Kyo."

"OK now all together say, 'Nam Myo Ho Ren Ge Kyo.'"

Christopher began busting up, "Vietnam, Santa Claus is a fagot in Tokyo."

"Come on you goof ball, just say it once all the way through, right. I know you can do it. Say, 'Nam Myo-ho Ren-ge Kyo.'"

"What does it mean?"

"Come on just try it once, and I'll tell you what it means."

"OK. How do you say it again?"

"Nam Me-Yo Ho Ren Gay Key-Yo." This time Debussy really enunciated each syllable.

"Na Me Ho Ray Ko."

"Almost. It's Nam Myo Ho Ren Ge Kyo."

"OK you're gonna tell me what I'm saying right?"

"Of course. Just try it first, 'Nam Myo Ho Ren Ge Kyo.'"

"Nam Myo Ho," Christopher repeated slowly.

Debussy joined in, "Ren Ge Kyo."

Christopher mimicked slowly, "Ren Ge Kyo."

"Good. You did it." They were both laughing loudly now and smiling just as much as they did that first day of school in their underground clubhouse. And they didn't even need to take any drugs. "See I told you it makes you feel real good inside."

"I'm just happy to see you again. It sucks hangin' out with Nathan lately. He's turned into such an asshole."

"Oh, he has always been a little bit of an asshole." They continued laughing as Debussy tried to explain what Christopher had just said.

Theodore warned Debussy not to get too philosophical or theoretical. He said it's like a television engineer trying to explain to a person who has never seen a television, how it works. If the engineer goes into all the technical aspects of how the television transmits sound and picture from one place to another, and all the other intricacies of how a television functions mechanically, it would really do the person little good, if they never turned the TV on, and saw it for themselves. The person who has never watched a TV would benefit more from just turning the TV on, while not knowing how it works.

Theodore said it's better to let someone try chanting and experience it for oneself. That would be much more impressive to them than all the Buddhist philosophy. Then once they understand it, through experiencing it benefiting their life, they can go into studying it deeper. On the other hand, if someone studies and studies, but never tries chanting, they will never know exactly how it can benefit their life. Buddhism emphasizes actual proof, along with documentary and theoretical proof. Some religions, all they can offer for proof is a book someone wrote many hundreds of years ago. And people are asked to have faith in something that can't be proven. Nichiren Buddhism on the other hand asks someone to simply try chanting, and doesn't ask that person to believe in it, until that person sees the benefits. Once someone sees the results, that person will naturally develop faith in the practice.

But Debussy just couldn't see how he could get his friend to try chanting, without giving him a thorough explanation of what it meant. And as he was not skilled at being brief, he of course went way over board, and gave a complete explication, that would even wear out some Buddhist philosophers.

Debussy tried relating the chant to two books he had been reading about quantum mechanics, called *The Dancing Wu Li Masters*, and *The Seat of the Soul*, along with many other things he had been studying. If he could relate it to things that didn't seem religious, perhaps he wouldn't turn Christopher away from it.

"So 'Nam' is a Japanese word that comes from a Sanskrit word. It's an abbreviated form of Namu, which signifies devotion or a fusion of one's life with something or someone. Have you ever seen the big dot some Indian women have on the center of their foreheads?"

"Yeah." He giggled, "So am I saying something about Indian women?"

"No silly. It just comes from the same word root. An Indian wears that to either signify her devotion to or fusion with her husband, as in a marriage. Or if she's not married, it can have religious significance-representing her devotion to her god or faith."

"OK. What does the rest mean?"

"Alright, 'Myo-Ho' represents the physical and spiritual manifestations of life."

"Wow big words. What have you turned into Einstein on me?"

"Oh come on; don't be stupid. I've been reading a little, and studying with my friend, Theodore."

"Who's Theodore? Does he go to our school?"

"No he was a friend of my dads. He used to work with him on educational radio programs."

"Dude, your dad was on the radio? What station?"

"He was on Pacifica Radio."

"I never heard of that station."

"It was started after World War II in Berkeley, California, as a peace activist station. 'Pacifica' means peace."

"Are they still around today?"

"Yes. It has grown into a large network of progressive stations that focus on education, culture and peace. They still have their original station up in Berkeley, KPFA. Then in Los Angeles they have KPFK, 90.7 FM. They also have stations in Texas, Washington DC, and New York. You can also listen to all of their stations on the internet at www.pacifica.org. The LA one is the one my dad and Theodore were on. Theodore's still on that station at night.

"The goal of the station is to bridge gaps between different cultures, religions, and ideas, and to provide a medium free of moneyed interests. That's why it's completely listener funded. They don't take any money from corporations, nor have any commercials. So they are completely free to report the news as it is, without having to cater to their advertisers. It's really cool. You'll hear things that will never be played on corporate owned stations. They tell you things big business and the government wouldn't want you to know."

"So what does your friend do on that station?"

"Oh, he's a late night show host. He does a show on spirituality and Eastern philosophy. I've listened to it a few times. It's pretty cool."

"You sound like you know a lot about it."

"Oh, a little bit."

"So is this where you heard about this chant thing?"

"No, I read it in some of my dad's books, which I found in our garage."

"So you were telling me what the rest of that chant means, before we got off the subject." Christopher put him back on track.

"Oh yeah, so 'Myo-ho' signifies the Law of life which manifest itself as both physical and spiritual reality. The literal translation of 'Myo-ho' is 'Wondrous Law.' But to understand it better, I think it is good to understand the first three of the ten factors of life according to Shakyamuni."

"Who the heck is Shakazuli?"

"It's Shakyamuni. He was a prince in India, back some 500 to 1000 years before Christ. His birth name was Siddhartha. But anyway, I'll tell you more about him another time. The first three factors of life are 'Appearance, Nature, and Entity.'

"'Appearance' is everything that has physical form, which you can see. Some western philosophers, scientists, and doctors believe everything comes down to its physical make up. They even go as far as saying love is just a chemical reaction. They believe that beyond the chemicals nothing exists. This is the Western pragmatic reductionist view of life. It's very one sided. People who believe this way think you can change anything by changing its physical make up. They think if a person is suffering from depression they can simply give that person some chemical to make up for a chemical their body isn't producing, because they are depressed. Little do they know, the lack of chemical in their body is a physical manifestation of the entity of their life, which is in a state of depression, and unless you change the entity, you won't change the problem. It's like trying to change a shadow; it won't change the object that is projecting the shadow.

"Then there are those, mainly in the East who think everything is made up of thoughts and energies, which corresponds to the factor of 'Nature.' These people think that even the atom when reduced down past its electrons, protons, and neutrons, down even past quarks and leptons, is only a pattern of organic energy, a form of thought they say. Well the materialists and the spiritualists are both basically right, from their own vantage point. But it is as if two blind people were touching an elephant, one on the tail and the other on the trunk. Both would describe what they think an elephant looks like. And both would be correct in describing that little part of the elephant, but it wouldn't describe the elephant in its entirety.

"Now quantum mechanics, which is a branch of physics explains how reality exhibits both of these qualities. For instance Einstein and his contemporaries were puzzled by the fact that light, under one set of experiments, proves to be a particle, called a photon, which represents the factor of 'appearance.' Yet under different experiments, light proved to be a wave, which is a thought-form, which represents the factor of 'nature,' or the spiritual manifestation of life.

"Western scientists had a problem with this dualism, but in the East this wasn't too much of a problem. Yet Einstein was neither satisfied with the particle theory, nor the wave theory. He spent much of his later years searching for what he called the 'Unifying Field Theory,' which would explain and unify both cosmic laws and quantum laws and even the laws of the physical and spiritual realms. Einstein of course wanted to quantify it, or come up with the mathematical equation that explains this 'unifying field.'

"Little did these scientists know that Shakyamuni explained this unifying theory in the last eight years of his life, in a set of teaching called the 'Teaching of the Lotus of the Wondrous Law,' or the Lotus Sutra. In the second chapter of this sutra, called the Expedient Means Chapter, Shakyamuni some 2,500-3000 years ago explained that life is an 'entity' that manifests itself both spiritually and physically, and it is neither too big to encompasses the smallest particle, nor too small to encompass the vastness of the entire universe. So life is neither physical nor spiritual, but manifests itself as both. Similarly, light is neither a wave nor a particle, but manifests as both. This 'entity of life' is The Wondrous Law, or 'Myo-ho.'"

"Wow that's pretty deep. But strangely enough it makes perfect sense to me." Now Christopher was getting really interested. "So what about the rest?"

Debussy continued getting very excited that his friend was willing to listen. This philosophizing gave him great joy. He was dying to tell people all he had been reading lately. So of course he couldn't stop. "OK 'Ren Ge' is the characters for lotus blossom. The lotus blossom has a lot of symbolism. It was the most prestigious flower of ancient India and much of Asia. It was the symbol of royalty. They would sprinkle lotus blossoms on the ground to signify the path the king and queen would walk, when entering a formal ceremony. It was no wonder Shakyamuni decided to use the lotus blossom as the symbol for his highest teaching, which is the king of teachings. It was the very pinnacle of everything he was trying to teach over his more than fifty years of teaching. It was the essence and the main purpose of his whole existence."

Debussy went on ad nauseum. "The lotus blossom also symbolizes purity within impurity. The lotus is a flower that blooms out of a muddy swamp. It is fabled that the muddier the swamp the more beautiful the lotus blossom."

"Ah huh." Nathan feverishly tried to stretch his brain, to absorb the plethora of information Debussy was spewing from his mouth.

"It was prophesied that the Lotus Sutra would spread during a muddied kalpa, or a time of great impurity, a time of chaos much like we live in today. At this time the 'Bodhisattvas of the Earth,' which are those people, who would practice the Lotus Sutra would rise from the ground, and bloom like beautiful lotus blossoms. Of course it's just an analogy of people bringing out their greatness under the worst of circumstances.

"The lotus blossom also symbolizes the simultaneous nature of the law of cause and effect, as it relates to someone's life. The lotus blossom is one of the few flowers that casts its seeds out at the same time that it blooms. What this represents is when someone awakens to his or her highest potential, they instantly cast out seeds, which become planted in other people's lives. So they too will awaken to their highest potential.

"Finally the word, 'Kyo' means, 'sutra,' which is an Indian word meaning 'teaching.' It is said there are some eighty thousand sutras, or different teaching that Shakyamuni taught-one for each of the eighty thousand sufferings that people have. But of all the sutras, the Lotus

Sutra was the only one that was not for his time, nor for the people of India where he lived. He even didn't preach it for his highest and most trusted successors. When they asked if they could be the votaries of the Lotus Sutra and spread it to all the people, he refuses their request. And instead he said that in a time in the distant future, some two thousand years or more, there would be a teacher greater than he born, who would lead the people in spreading the Lotus Sutra, eventually to the entire world, and bring peace to all people."

"So when would that be?" Christopher was very interested.

Debussy continued, "This was believed to be during the 1200's. A man named Nichiren was born who fulfilled the prophecies of the Lotus Sutra."

"How come we haven't seen peace yet?"

"Well unfortunately, it hasn't been easy to spread the teaching in the Lotus Sutra. There has been great persecution waged against people who try to spread it. Nichiren was the greatest example of this. He was banished many times. And many people including the government in Japan tried to kill him. But fortunately he survived. But his teachings didn't really start spreading worldwide until about the 1960's. Now there are roughly twelve million people in about one hundred, ninety countries practicing his teachings. And it is growing. And I believe it will be one of the many things that will bring peace to the world."

"Well everyone sure hopes something will. But who knows?"

"Well we can only see, but for me I've found peace in myself, which is a start. Anyway, as I was saying, the character used for 'Kyo' is not like the other character's normally used for 'sutra.' It is like writing 'Kyo' with a capital 'K,' to signify that it is the king of sutras, or the sutra of sutras. So all together we can say, 'Nam Myo-ho Ren-ge Kyo' means: devotion to or fusion with the 'King Sutra of the Wondrous Law of the Lotus Blossom.'"

"Wow that sounds neat. You sure know a lot about it. And you seem so excited about it. And you seem so much different from the last time I hung out with you."

"Yeah, I've been reading a lot about it and chanting it the way Tina Turner does in that movie, so I can bring out my highest potential."

Debussy got Christopher to try chanting for a while. And then they went on talking until it started to get dark. They laughed and reminisced. Debussy felt so happy. He had wanted to share what he had learned with someone. And now he was finally able to do so. He couldn't stop talking once he started. There was so much he had read, and what good would it do, if he kept it all bottled up inside. The lessons of life have to be passed on. He couldn't hoard all the wealth of information he had been filling himself with. He also was realizing that helping others was the surest road to happiness. The happiness he gained by trying to give happiness to others seemed to feel so much more fulfilling.

Ten States of Life

When he got home that night he felt so alive. He went up and down through the whole cycle of possible feelings that day, as if he were on a roller coaster. At school he felt tranquil most of the day, although occasionally he was in a state of hunger, whenever he saw a cute girl whom he desired. And then as he met with his friend, he felt glad to see him. But suddenly he became sad when he heard their clubhouse had been destroyed, and when he thought about not being able to go to the beach, and how he would miss his town when he moved away. From that moment and leading up to it, it was as if the happy feelings had vanished into nowhere, and in their stead feelings of loss entered his heart. Where did those feelings of joy go?

And then when he went to Christopher's house, his depression evaporated, and he momentarily transgressed back to a state of hunger, as he felt a little jealous by the beautiful home that Christopher lived in, which he could only have dreams of. However, once he became aware of his state of hunger, he was by some force of will able to lift himself out of this longing state. Once he rose above the hunger, he was able to direct his life to an even higher state. But where did those hungry feelings go? They evaporated as he began to explain Buddhism to his friend. Once he felt a sense of compassion to teach his friend, he realized that regardless of the great house Christopher lived in, he was still not happy. At that moment Debussy felt the desire to eradicate his friend's sufferings, and give him joy. Once he started trying to teach his friend, he became filled with a sense of elation. But then where did the depression go, once the joy became manifested?

He had been learning from Ho Goku's books, and from Theodore that the different states of life one experiences could be controlled. One didn't have to be tossed endlessly from a state of utter despair, to a state of insatiable desire, to a state of rapture and then back down again, like a ship trying to cross the sea of suffering. One could raise whatever state they are in instantly, and feel a sense of peace and happiness.

As Debussy was learning, Buddhism categorized the different emotional states a person could experience into ten categories-the lowest being "Hell," or utter despair, and the highest being "Enlightenment," or a state of complete wisdom, total compassion, unlimited happiness and boundless freedom. It categorizes the states most people go through on a regular basis, as the "Six Lower Paths." In these six states a person is at the mercy of their environment. At one moment they can feel joy, and at the next they can feel great inner turmoil, when circumstances turn unfavorable to them.

Debussy learned that in early Buddhist teachings these states were taught as different worlds. And people practicing these early teachings actually believed there were separate worlds you go to for different states. This is where the early ideas of heaven and hell, existing in a place other than the Earth came from. But most people who have truly experienced great despair or immense joy know that they don't have to go anywhere. Their whole life in those states becomes a world of either heaven or hell.

The same holds true of the other four lower paths. What was once believed to be a separate land where hungry spirits sucked the life-force from people, was later seen as a state-of-being, where one feels completely controlled by their desires. Their desires eat at them like hungry spirits. And they never feel satisfied in this state, which Buddhism calls "Hunger."

What was once thought to be a land where only animals lived, where the laws of the jungle reigned, became known as a state of selfishness, where one only thinks of fulfilling one's own desires, even at the expense of others. This state, Mahayana, or "The Higher Vehicle" Buddhisms call the state of "Animality." A corporate executive who lays off thousands of people for stock options is in this state.

What was once thought by Theravada Buddhism, or what Mahayana Buddhists call "Hinayana," meaning "Lower Vehicle" Buddhisms to be a land of angry spirits, called "Ashuras," was later seen as a state-of-mind where one feels deep rage and hatred toward others. This state became known as the state of "Anger." A president who sends troops to bomb a neutral country is in this state.

What was once thought to be a land of human beings, who lived peacefully, became known as the state of "Tranquility" or "Humanity," which one feels when they neither feel pain nor joy. A drunken person can experience this state, but like all the six lower states, it is transient. Eventually they will become sober.

Debussy read in *Life; an Enigma a Precious Jewel*, that one could think of these different states of life as originating from how much our vital life-force is either activated or drained. When we are full of vital life-force, we feel more peaceful. We are more satisfied. We are not as controlled by our surroundings, and we are in a higher life-state.

From the lowest state of life: "Hell," one can raise to "Hunger," to "Animality," "Anger" or "Tranquility," as their life-force becomes more charged with energy. Although through the dynamic pulsating rhythms of life, one does not always move in a steady direction from "Hell" to "Hunger." One can be in "Animality" one instance, and the next suddenly be in "Heaven." Then the next that person could plunge to "Hell." In these six states, many things in one's environment act as external stimuli to either activate their life-force or sap their life-force.

Most people as Debussy was learning, are drawn more often to their basic state or tendency, when no external stimulus is present. For some, that could be "Tranquility," if they are by nature a humane person, or "Hell" if they are naturally a very weak hearted person, who is often always in a state of complete destructiveness and despair. Someone who goes on a shooting spree, and then takes his or her own life, can be said to be manifesting the life state of "Hell."

But as one learns to control one's life-force, and actively manifest it, their tendency begins to be elevated. So that without even having something in their environment that would make them feel happy, they just instinctively feel elated. And eventually they can even transcend these six lower states, and begin directing their self along a higher path.

When one's life becomes strong enough, they can free themselves momentarily from the many external stimuli of their environment. Then they can begin to attain the freedom to direct their life in the direction toward "Enlightenment." This is another name for absolute freedom. On their journey, some may feel a desire to enrich their life. They will manifest the life-state of "Learning," in which they will be drawn to learn from the wisdom of others. Or they may open up to their own inherent wisdom, and enter along the path of "Realization." But as their life-force becomes even more manifest, the most natural state, which is one with the law of life, emerges. That is the life-state of compassion, which Buddhism calls the state of "Altruism" or "Bodhisattva." This is realized when someone awakens to the fact that all life is inner-connected. One in this state of "Altruism" realizes that what benefits others, naturally benefits oneself, and what harms others also harms oneself. In this compassionate state one derives joy from imparting happiness to others. And when others suffer, they too feel the suffering and offer encouragement to those in need. If a corporate executive were in this state of life, he would see that shutting down a car factory, to move it to a place where they can get away with paying people below poverty wages, will only cause them in the long run to not have enough people who could afford their cars, then they would see that the move is a loss for them, as much as it is a loss to their workers, who are inter-connected with them. They wouldn't be fooled by the short-term gains, and blind to the long-term losses, caused by selfishness.

These three vehicles, "Learning," "Realization" and "Altruism" are also subject to change and external influences-yet less so than the lower paths. And unlike the lower paths, in these states, one has a positive effect on one's environment. Even though one may be able to manifest on their own the "the Higher Vehicles," and for some these are by nature their normal states (Such people as Einstein are by nature in the state of "Realization" and people like Mother Theresa are by nature in the state of "Altruism"). Not all of us have these states as our natural tendency. Some of us have to call these states into manifestation. For those, Debussy was learning, calling forth the "Wondrous Law of the Lotus Blossom" seemed to be the surest way to bringing these latent states into being.

The key Debussy found is to activate this Wondrous Law of Life as often as possible, by invoking it, by simply saying aloud, "Nam Myo-ho Ren-ge Kyo," for this is the name of the Tenth State of Life, which everyone possesses, although it is often completely dormant. Just like nuclear energy, which has always existed inside an atom, which took an enlightened person to discover the formula to unleash this dormant energy, Nichiren simply discovered the formula, which was hidden in the Lotus Sutra. The Five Characters that form the title of the Lotus Sutra in Chinese/Japanese characters are Myo Ho Ren Ge Kyo. In the same way the five character formula "E Equals M C Squared ($E=mc^2$)" unlocked a riddle, which was always inherent in life, the five characters of the Lotus Sutra, unlocked an even stronger force-a force of absolute wisdom, and boundless compassion-that once manifested frees a person from the chains of karma. No longer does one have to be a cog in the wheel of capitalism. No longer does one have to conform to a hierarchy that says: kings are higher than priests; priests are higher than merchants; merchants are higher than peasants. Once one realizes that they are the makers of their own reality, they do not have to conform to some outmoded construct, which was invented to control people, and to justify the exploitation of one group of people over another. This is real freedom! In the same way the formula that released the neutrons and the protons from the nucleus, this formula of the Lotus Sutra can release every human being from the slavery they have been taught to conform to.

Debussy was beginning to believe this was the only way to rectify the contradictions of society, and bring peace to the world. As many people as possible had to realize fully their inner power, and begin using that power in a positive way to make progressive changes in the world. As Debussy read in the SCV's monthly newspaper, the *World Tribune*, "Once the people lead, the leaders will follow." The only reason the leaders of the world were able to abuse their power, was because the people felt powerless to stop them. They had been convinced even before the Roman Empire that some greater power lied somewhere outside of them. And they constantly gave away their own power to this external social construct. The only reason corporations were able to use people like cogs in the wheel and exploit them, others and even nature, was because people felt powerless to stop them. Debussy was beginning to see that the exploited were just as much to blame as the exploiters, for not taking back their own power, which they were constantly giving up to big businesses and corrupt governments, for a false sense of security.

Debussy saw that this was much more prevalent in the so-called "Third World," where the "all embracing" Roman faith had been forced upon the people, to subdue their own powers, so that they could be completely controlled. It was a philosophy like Buddhism that was so needed to re-empower the people to take control of their governments, their economies, and their world. However, it must first start as an inner change, and each person has to take control of their life-state and be in control of their desires and feelings and raise their life-state to that of compassion.

***

When Debussy woke up the next morning he felt so great. He had never thought of writing poetry, nor did he really care for poetry, until he started reading Ho Goku's poems. But how he felt that morning while chanting, he had to somehow share with others. So he penned these words:

The Celebration of Life

As I awoke this morning, I inhaled the cool morning air
And exhaled the warm breath from within.

I felt so alive.
As I drank the Earth's water,
I sensed the flow of life-force to every cell of my body.
As I ate the fruits of the Earth,
I metabolized new energy for growth-for new life.
The warmth of the sun that showed through the shades
Warmed my face, and once again
I chanted the "Wondrous Law of the Lotus Blossom-
Nam Myo-ho Ren-ge Kyo!"
I chanted in celebration of my symbiotic union with the macrocosms.
For I am a microcosm of Air, Water, Earth, Fire and Consciousness.
'Twas not a new month, nor new year today.
'Twas not a new century, nor new millennium.
No fragment of eternity caused me celebration.
I celebrate in spite of those who wish I would mourn.
I need not a birthday cake, a Christmas tree,
An Easter egg, nor bottle of wine.
Nor do I need the birth or death of any "great man,"
To enjoin my celebration.
I celebrate life in spite of those who wish I would mourn.
My life is a celebration, and your life too is a celebration-
'Tis the celebration of billions and billions of years of evolution.
No, an eternity of evolution-for we are the Lotus Blossoms.
As I bloom, I cast my seeds out to you,
"Nam Myo-ho Ren-ge Kyo."

-Debut X

Reunited

As Debussy invoked the law, he thought of all the people in his life-all the people he wanted someday to feel as happy as he felt now-his mom, his brother, his deceased father, his friends-even those he'd forgotten. Suddenly they came back from his memory. Then his drifting mind landed on that cute girl at that gigantic bookstore he visited at the beginning of the year.

"Man, what was her name?" He could picture her bending down to search the shelves, which he already knew contained no books he was looking for. He forgot all about her until just now. Often many unexplained things would wander into his mind while chanting-things he would have never thought of without calling forth his enlightened nature.

"Damn, I wonder if she still works there?" He thought, as he continued chanting. "I should go there sometime and see her again. She must like books as much as I do, to want to work in a bookstore?"

After school he took the bus there. He took the escalator to the top floor, got a cup of tea from the coffeehouse inside. He made his way to the "Eastern Philosophy" section, sipping on his warm hot ginkgo and ginseng tea.

He looked through the books. And to his amazement there were four Ho Goku books staring straight out at him. *Before It's Too Late, Space and Eternal Life*, *A Search for a New Humanity,* and *Dawn After Dark*. These were dialogues Ho Goku had published with leading world figures. One was with the founder of The Club of Rome. One was with a leading Sri Lankan astronomer. Another was with a professor of philosophy at the University of Bonn, in Germany. And the last was with an art critic and member of the *Acedemie Francaise*.

While he was looking through the books, a girl asked if he needed any help finding anything. He looked up to the beautiful brunette he'd spoken to before. She was wearing dark, tight dress pants, with medium heals, and a button up blouse that clung to her beautifully. "Hi. I was in here about six months ago, and I was searching for books by Ho Goku. But you didn't have any. Now I see you have four."

"Hey that's right. You're the one. I owe you big time. I've been reading his books since you turned me on to his writings. I requested a bunch of them be ordered for the store. We have a lot more.

I've been saying that phrase he talks about, 'Nam My Oh Ho Ren Gee Key Yo.' Or something like that."

"You almost got it right." Debussy smiled. "That's pretty good. Actually it's Nam Myo-ho Ren-ge Kyo." He said laughing.

"Well they didn't have any frickin' pronunciation guide in those books." She laughed back.

"I know. You should come to one of the introduction meetings. They teach you how to say it there."

"What? They have meetings around here?" She exclaimed. "I thought it was only in Japan?"

"It started there. But now it's all over. In Southern California alone there are about thirty thousand people practicing it. They have about thirty district meetings just in Orange County. And they are opening a new university in Orange County larger than the one they have in LA."

"No way! All this time I've been struggling on my own to say it, and I've wished someone could help me. And all this time there's been people all around who do this?"

"You're lucky, it's only been six months or so. Some people wait their whole life. And still they don't stumble upon anything this great."

"I guess you're right. Are you gonna be here a while."

"Yeah. Why?" He asked.

"Well I'm supposed to go on my lunch break now. But I want to talk to you more." Debussy wanted to talk to her too.

"I can stay as long as you'd like me to." He smiled.

"Cool. Do you want to go to lunch with me? And we can talk more." She asked.

"Sure. It's kind of late for me to have lunch. But I'd love to keep you company."

"Great." She clocked out and they went out into the mall, to the food area.

She got her food, and they sat in the shade of a tree. "You know what I've been most interested in, in reading Ho Goku's books, is the 'Nine Levels of Consciousness.' I've always thought maybe I'd study to become a psychologist or para-psychologist, when I go to college. So much of what I've been reading about that subject parallels what Ho Goku writes about Buddhism."

"Oh yeah!" Debussy got excited; here was something he could easily have a conversation with her about. "Have you read Dr. Weiss's books?"

"Oh my god, he's my favorite author!" She smiled brightly. "I've read, *Many Lives Many Masters*, *Through Time Into Healing*, and *Only Love is Real.*"

"No way, I've read those books too. Well I've always thought the 'Nine Levels of Consciousness' was a very interesting way of explaining how consciousness manifests. Buddhism calls the ninth level, Myo-ho, or the Wondrous Law. This is so much like Jung's idea of 'Universal Consciousness' huh? At this level 'all is one.' There is no separation between different conscious beings, at the core of life. Every change in consciousness has an effect on the entire universe. On our first six levels of consciousness, which is our five senses plus our normal conscious waking mind, we perceive a separation. But no separation really exists. " Debussy loved philosophizing. If someone gave him the time, he would rattle on all day.

"It's so amazing that a prince of a small tribe in ancient India would realize all of this." She was getting into the conversation so much that she hardly ate any of her food. "Now it seems modern thinkers are only beginning to approach his level of insight."

"Well they say, after giving up on all the teachers of his time, because what they were trying to teach him didn't answer the questions he had, he finally went off to meditate by himself for some time. It is there that he recalled the lessons of all of his hundreds of past lives, and all the spiritual teachers he had studied under. In the way Dr. Weiss is able to perform past live regressions, by performing hypnosis on his patients, Siddhartha performed a sort of self-hypnosis, I believe. Since more and more prominent psychologists are now using this technique on their patients to unearth and resolve hidden subconscious ailments, what Siddhartha said about seeing hundreds of lives back in an instance doesn't seem too improbable.

"In relation to the Eighth Level of Consciousness or the Karmic Storage Level, as they call it, I think that although one can expiate negative memory on the normal subconscious level, which is the Seventh Level of Consciousness, by doing past life regressions, like Dr. Weiss does, and many other psychologists, I believe chanting is the fastest way to expunge all of the many life times of negative causes we have made, which are stored on this eighth level, which is our karma. By calling forth our ninth level of consciousness, or this pure energy of life, as they call it: Myo-ho Ren-ge Kyo, we clean out all of the other levels of consciousness. I hate to say it while you're eating, but it's kind of like getting a conscious enema."

"Oh I think I'm done eating now." She just laughed at his analogy, and listened attentively, with a big grin on her face. "Or it's like defragmenting your hard drive."

"Yes." He liked this one; he was a little upset he didn't already think of the analogy himself. "So you see, we wash out all the crap that has been accumulating in the deep recesses of our consciousness, so that not only do we think more clearly, with out any karmic biases, and subconscious conditionings, but we also begin to see reality for what it is. And more importantly, we are able to see *ourselves*-which is the most difficult. And we can actually see what we are doing that prevents us from being happy, and living a life of complete fulfillment and satisfaction."

"Wow that's incredible. God I wish I didn't have to get back to work now. I want to maybe go to one of those Buddhist introduction meetings with you. Or just talk to you more away from work."

Debussy was excited. They exchanged numbers, and he walked her back to the bookstore and said bye. They both smiled and as he was about to leave, she gave him a big hug. It felt so good to him; he had rarely been hugged by any girls his age. He didn't want to let go. But he did, and they departed.

The Last Day

The last day of school seemed to come quicker than Debussy expected. As he left his final class, he went to turn in his books and clean out his locker. The sun was shining so bright on the square. He had said good-bye to his friends, and the teachers he liked most. He would no longer be a freshman; he didn't know whether to feel happy or sad. He knew there were things he'd miss, and then others he'd be glad to put behind him.

He put his supplies in his backpack and left the locker bays. He walked through the square and came upon Officer Sajack, who seemed melancholy. Debussy never said hi to him, and he was sure few others did either. But for the first time he felt sorry for Sajack. So he did the unexpected, "Hey Officer Sajack, take care man, enjoy your summer." He was amazed by how good it made him feel.

Sajack looked up in amazement, and a smile came to his face, "Hey thanks; you too."

Debussy thought to himself, "He's not such a bad guy, I'm sure."

As he was crossing the lawn, entering Main Street, he heard a sweet voice call from behind, "Debut!"

With surprise, he turned around to the unexpected-flowing light brown hair, and beautiful smile, the daughter of the city mayor herself, Lori Thompson. She ran up to him, "Hey Debut. I wanted to say I enjoyed your writings that you shared in English class."

"Thank you." He was flattered and flustered at the same time.

"I liked how you compared what the Romans did with Christ's name, to what the United States did to the word 'democracy.' The more I thought about it, the more it made sense. The common people of Rome admired Jesus as a rebel against the ruling elites, so facing overwhelming protest from the people, the government finally decided to steal his name for their own made up dogma. In one of my papers I wrote about the novel *1984*, where Orwell imagined that by 1984 England will have twisted the words, "peace," "freedom" and "strength" so badly that their slogan becomes, 'War Is Peace; Freedom is Slavery; Ignorance is Strength.' Similarly, it seams that many Christians in the US today have changed the commandment, 'Thou shall not kill,' into 'Thou shall kill.'

"It was just like during the forming of the US constitution. The elite rulers in the US were facing insurmountable opposition from the people to have democracy, and although they never supported the idea, they thought if they used the name 'democracy' they could fool the people into believing they really had it."

Debussy walked across the grass, excited to be talking to her. "Those who rule the language can twist it for their own benefit. It seems the Soviet Union did the same thing with the word 'Communism,' a great political ideology in and of itself. But they called their government 'Communist,' because the people were protesting change and wanted a communal society. But the elites didn't do anything to make their government represent the ideals in Marx's Communist Manifesto. They simply stole the name."

"That makes perfect sense." Lori said, "Just change the words to mean anything you want, and you can fool the people into believing you've given them what they've asked for. Kind of like what our government did with words like 'freedom' and 'free trade.'"

"Exactly!" Debussy agreed.

"You know how I always have a tape recorder in class to help me take notes? I've listened many times to your reports. And I found them very informative. I never got a chance to tell you that I especially liked that report you read about Nichiren. I've been looking for some books about him. But I haven't had any luck finding them."

Debussy took a deep breath, and with a big grin he replied, "Thanks. I had the same problem before. You can't find books about him anywhere, it seems."

"No!" She nodded in approval, still smiling.

"Luckily I met a guy who has lots of his writings, and many other books about him. He's let me borrow them. I'm sure he wouldn't mind also loaning some to you."

"Well I can buy them from him as well."

"Yeah, or he can purchase them for you from LA, where he works."

"That would be great. My dad couldn't pick me up today, so I'm walking home. I've seen you pass my house before. I live right by Lake Park. I remember one day you were wrestling with your friends in the grass. You guys were making so much noise that I had to peek out the curtains of my bedroom to see what was going on. At the time, I didn't yet know who you were."

"Wow you live right there. I walk that way all the time."

"Yeah, I live in that green, Victorian house by the benches."

"Oh, I know that one. Wow, that's a beautiful house! I never knew you lived there."

"Yeah, do you mind if I walk with you."

"Ah, sure. I mean no. I mean, I wouldn't mind if you walked with me. That would be great." He tried to contain his glee-not that well though.

She smiled again, and he smiled too.

As they began walking to the crosswalk Lori sighed, "God, it's a beautiful day today, huh?"

Debussy thought, "What's God got to do with it." But he refrained. Instead he said, "Yeah, isn't it."

The sun also seemed to smile in the sky. There were no clouds in sight.

Afterword

(When Timothy first finished writing this book in 2000, before he attended Soka University of America, he wrote the following as a foreword. However, now we feel it has become a little outdated, so we offer it instead as an afterword.)

Much of what we define as the fabric of reality is actually a fabrication. Many feel that what has been termed "the Information Era," is in fact an "Era of Misinformation." With this in mind, I dedicate this book to the tens of thousands of young and motivated people (human rights, environmental and labor activists and organizers,) who showed up in Seattle, December 1999, Washington DC, April 2000, and once again during the summer 2000 political conventions, to voice their opposition to an out-of-control transnational, corporate, so-called "free market" system. For these youths who are attempting to see through all the propaganda and lies, I hope to offer some alternative worldviews and philosophies, that I believe can help in solving the growing crises they are being forced to confront.

This novel is an attempt to battle the mounting greed based, Western material culture, which has at its roots a false and obsolete, Roman worldview. This Roman worldview promotes human domination over nature, unrestrained greed and privileged elite's control over the masses. (Though these views are older than Rome, I call them "Roman," because Rome under Constantine and others help crystallize these views and make them world recognized and accepted-under the cloak of an "all embracing" religion.)

Myth Shattering tries to debunk the notion that these erroneous ideologies have any connection to the Nazarene, whom the Eastern world knew as "Prince Issa," during his 17 year travels there as a young crusader of human rights and social justice, and to the Essenes as "Essa," their "Teacher of Righteousness." Yes like those young activists who staged mass protest rallies at the two-party duopoly's corporate sponsored conventions in 2000, Jesus too was a protester.

This book offers the enlightened perspectives of such Eastern revolutionaries, as the young prince of the Shakya Tribe, from that great millennium before the rise of Constantine's bishops in Rome, who single-mindedly dealt a powerful blow to the caste system of India, proclaiming that all beings, sentient and insentient are equally deserving of respect. It also offers the stories of such courageous worriers of justice, as the monk of 13th century Japan, Nichiren, who stood up to the Shogunate of Kamakura, to declare a correct and egalitarian view of Siddhartha's most enlightened teachings.

I offer this novel to young Earth Firsters, Fair Traders, Anarchists, and Ruckus Society advocates-to give them some hope that they can surmount the Mickey Mouse Club, multinational profiteers, who hope to transform our world's last resources into a McHeaven, for their shareholders. I try to demonstrate that the ideas of the revolutionaries of the past can empower youths of today to win over the pillagers from Wall Street. In addition, I strive to show how these ancient philosophers' views are very much inline with the values and concerns of today's youth, and how they can use them as guiding principals to steer us out of our current global malaise. I also hope to show the youth of the world, how these ancient freedom fighter's beliefs, are more congruent with the views of today's fighters of peace and democracy, such as Father Roy Bourgeois, Noam Chomsky, Helen Caldicott, and even Ralph Nader, than any other belief system offered in the known history of humanity.

Because not all of my young compatriots are bookworms, who will likely take the time to read a how-to textbook on grass roots democracy, I hope to reach out to them somehow, through an entertaining, semi-autobiographical journey of a young radical rebellious punk rocker, who desperately searches for a true "light at the end of the tunnel" of life. I try to use the language these kids use, and to look at life from their perspective.

Therefore, as a warning, if views that are contrary to your own, which may cause you to question your own past conditioning tend to offend you, you may find this book discomforting. On the other hand, if you want to expand your field of vision, to even for a moment look into the mind of one of today's X'ed out generation's hopeful idealists, than please follow him on his quest to discover reality, and find real individual freedom.

An Explanation of the Cover Art

When I first finished this novel in 2000, I hired an artist (unknown at the time), Michael Godard, who was working out of his apartment's garage in Huntington Beach, California, to paint the cover for my novel, before I searched for a publisher. During the painting of it, Michael Godard started to become better known, and eventually very famous. I had checked up with him from time to time, to see how the painting was coming along, and each time it became harder and harder to track him down, until finally he moved away from where I was living in Huntington Beach, into a small studio some cities away, only to move once again to an even bigger studio shortly after that.

The last time I saw him, at the small studio, I decided to pick up the painting, even though it wasn't completely finished, for fear I may never see him again, and also so I could make a copy of it, to send it to book publishers with my manuscript. When I picked it up, he promised he would finish it soon, whenever I brought it back to him.

During the same time, I began applying to the new Soka University of America in Aliso Viejo, California, where I was accepted in 2001 as a member of the 1st class of 120 students. The four years there were extremely busy, so I never got a chance to send out my novel to any other publishers, after an initial few submissions that yielded no responses. During my time at Soka University of America, I did manage to contact Michael Godard a few times by email, but he was now all over the world, and we were never able to find a time and a place where we could meet to have him finish the painting.

After I finally graduated Soka University in 2005, I've tried emailing him many times, but have yet to receive any replies. The painting in now in storage in San Diego, while I am living in Japan, so I hope someday we are in the same part of the world, and he will finish the cover painting as he promised and as I already paid him to do.

My original idea for the painting was to have a painting on a glass wall in the background, which represented a myth (the classical hierarchical societal myth of a five-tier society). There is a beggar in the foreground, representing workers and peasants. There is a merchant above him, representing the owning class. There is a church above that, representing the clergy or the holy class. Above that is the castle, where the rulers live, and above all that is heaven, represented by the circling angels and the clouds.

In the foreground, outside the glass wall painting, is Debussy Xanthankis, the main character of the novel, and he is throwing the book he wrote through the glass wall painting to shatter this myth. The yellow in the center is the unfinished shattering of the painting, which now looks more like a lightning bolt shattering Debussy's book. Through the shattered glass hole in the painting, sunlight is supposed to be streaming in on Debussy, representing the truth behind the lies of the myth.

At the time I hired Michael Godard to paint this novel cover, despite living in the grunge central of Orange County, he still sported a preppy/pretty boy hairdo and was not yet bedizened by tattoos. At the time he was painting incredible dream like fantasy paintings, which were so magical. Now, however, he has become a new person on an alcohol and gambling painting kick, and he has fully joined the star belly Sneetches of the world of fast cars and body art.

Though his paintings now are far less beautiful than his early works, he has found where the money is. Thus his website claims he is the "#1 Selling Artist in the World." I just hope in the process of finding money and fast cars, he has not lost his original creativity, and he can finish the cover of my novel before it becomes a best seller.

I'm sorry you are all not yet able to see the finished work.

Other Books by Timothy Harada
From Second American Renaissance Press

Second American Renaissance Press is a new, independent, non-profit publishing company, which will bring the writings of Soka University of America students to the world. Though graduates of Soka University of America founded Second American Renaissance Press, please note that Second American Renaissance Press is not an official publisher for Soka University of America and none of the books published by Second American Renaissance Press are official publications of Soka University of America.

Table of Contents

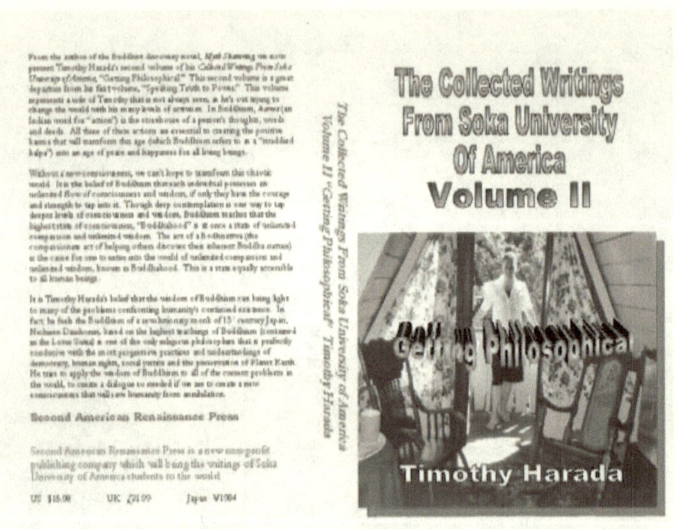

Table of Contents

Why are Juveniles Delinquent?
Nichiren the Buddha of Japan
A Revolution of Justice
The Evolution of Justice and Freedom
The Effects of Altruism
The Life of a Student
Trying to Understand My Beliefs
All We Have Is Our Words

Volume III Coming Soon:

The Least Unjust System
I am a Chandala and Proud of It
Who am I?
The Ignorance of Specialization
A More Enlightened Science
My Thoughts on Art and Activism
The Century of Women Has Now Begun at Soka University of America
It's a Damn Good Thing That Linus Pauling Didn't Teach at Soka University of America
Limits to Western Science
Western and Eastern Science
The Importance of Translation
The Arrogance of Western Materialism
It's All Been Done Before
The Meaning of Art?
Learning Humility
Studying SGI-USA
The Fallacy of Objectivity
A Celebration of Life
For the Love of Reading
A Time for Reflection Not Retaliation: *A letter to the Commander and Thief*
The Post Modern Effect
An Overview of My "Modes of Inquiry" Readings: *In a Disjunctive Modal Sort of Style?*
"Times They Are a-Changing" For Both Women and Men: *Fogle's assessment of "Young Goodman Brown"*
The Unfair World of Odysseus
Probing Beneath the Surface: *A deeper look at "To His Coy Mistress" and "The Love Song of J. Alfred Prufrock"*
The Aristotelian Critique of Sophocles

Cats and Golfing Make Flu Shots Easily Swallowed Over Tea Bags on Ice in the Late Afternoon
Reconstructing Sappho's Fragments
Huck's Transformation
The Greenpeace Warriors
The Complex Issues of the Civil War
I Am We
The 6th Year of My 6th, 6-Year Cycle
Literary Introductions
The Commodification of US Culture
The Geology and Geography of the Present-Day United States

Music by Timothy Harada

www.ingramcontent.com/pod-product-compliance
Lightning Source LLC
LaVergne TN
LVHW091004080826
845145LV00003B/1125

* 9 7 8 0 6 1 5 1 8 6 8 5 6 *